The Appalachian Trail

Over 2000 Smiles (and a few Groans)

Jack Darnell

Author of Sticky and Rags

ISBN:
ISBN-0981950795
ISBN-978-0-9819507-9-2

J & S Publications

DEDICATION

To my Wife Sherry, who said:

"We can hike the Appalachian Trail"

ACKNOWLEDGMENTS

Statistics are taken from public records and
personal experience.
The assistance in editing and proofing was
invaluable to the final publishing of this
book. My deepest appreciation to the
following:
JoAnn Trull
Evelyn Funderburk
Sherry Darnell

From the Author

My dear wife Sherry, decided to hike the Appalachian Trail (AT) late in life. She has followed my dreams and plans over much of the world with no complaint. One day I was talking about sailing around the world, her response was quick and serious. "No way, but why don't we hike the Appalachian Trail. It starts in Georgia and ends in Maine. We can do it." At the time, we were in our mid 60's. It was a challenge and the adventure of a life time. We fell short, but did manage over eighteen hundred and fifty miles of it, plus we did climb Katahdin.

The AT is the longest maintained foot path in the world! Last listed at 2170 miles. Through or touching 14 states. Each year over two thousand hardy hikers start the trek. Many do not make it more than two or three hundred miles. Some amazing people thru-hike (do the entire trail in one year, normally six or seven months). These hikers from all over the world come to face the challenge.

CHAPTER 1

Jerry was sitting in his easy chair reading an adventure novel, when he felt the love of his life, Sherry, as she squeezed past his book into his lap. "Okay, to what do I owe this sweet interruption?" he asked smiling.

"How does a picnic sound to you lover boy?" she said coyly.

"Is that right here or in the bedroom?" he said smiling as he pulled her close and got a kiss.

"Mind out of the gutter sir. I was thinking it has been a long time and the spring weather outside is calling us to the mountains."

"So that is the sweet voice I hear, spring weather," he said and he squeezed her tight. "You know, a ride and some of your fried chicken sounds like a winner sweetheart. When would you like to go, and what do I need to do?"

"You need to be only yourself Dr. Wiley, and be prepared to leave early in the morning, because you will probably awaken to the smell of fried chicken. I have the menu already set and we have it all here, no need to go to the store,"

Sherry said winking. She liked to wink. All her life she had wanted to wink, but had never learned the trick. She had mastered it now and used it in the sweetest ways. She had declared next she would learn to whistle. Never mind that it was a boy's thing. She had always wanted to whistle, now she was determined to learn.

One more kiss. This one a little longer and then she left him to his novel. As she walked away, his hand brushed her on the rear, "Nice pants Dr. Wiley." Jerry admired his wife's figure as she walked away. He thought to himself, as he had hundreds of times, *I was so stinking lucky to find this gem.* They were now in their mid-seventies and had been married just a few years. It was sort of a strange romance. They had known each other at Duke University where they had both graduated and then went their separate ways. He had never married and became Head of Duke Medical. Sherry had married another classmate and the newlyweds then began a practice in Huntersville, North Carolina.

Jerry was from a wealthy family in Pittsburgh and she from a mill hill family here in Mount Bell.

Jerry's wealth came from Wiley Industries, home based in Pittsburgh. Before marriage they had agreed to keep both homes. Jerry knew Sherry had deeper roots in Mount Bell so they had agreed to live there and commute to his home once a month for him to touch base. The home in Pittsburgh by today's standards was a mansion. It was fully staffed. In Mount Bell it was just the two of them.

The commute was now much faster with the new Gulfstream G650 the company had recently acquired. They had their own pilot, Stella, a sweet young lady who took care of the plane as if it were her own. The mechanic was Vickie and the girls lived in Gastonia in a loft apartment at the local airport where the jet was berthed.

Sherry's home, now their home, is located in the Hawthorne Subdivision in Mount Bell. It is a nice home and many in the community do not know their neighbor's net worth is over a billion dollars.

Jerry had lived a very colorful life away from Wiley Industries. He had been a CIA operative, the CEO of Wiley Industries and then organized a group he labeled the MVA (Modern Vigilante

Association). Jerry had always been a righteous individual. It bothered him when someone 'got away with murder' so to speak. So he formed a group that righted wrongs in society, with no fanfare and very seldom any violence. He was now retired and as the MVA bylaws read, it was to be disbanded at his death or retirement.

Now that he had found real love in his autumn years, he was thrilled to do things with this lovely lady. A picnic sounded good. His mind could not help but wander to the island of his dreams, the Greek Island of Corfu. He remembered while on assignment with the CIA watching the families on weekends walk the parks and spread picnics. Alone on a hotel balcony, he had longed to enjoy life as simply as those island folk. His life with the CIA was anything but simple.

Back to the present. He could hear things moving in the kitchen, so he marked his place and walked over to the bar that separated the kitchen from the small dining area, "Okay what can I do sweet lady?"

"I'm going to fix some potato salad in the morning. You can peel two potatoes if you still remember how to use a knife," she laughed pointing him to the potatoes.

As he peeled the potatoes, they talked about the exciting vacation they had enjoyed last year in the Mediterranean. They laughed at the fact they were ignoring his near death at the hands of terrorists. Jerry's mindset had always been *all's well that ends well,* and it had.

"I wish I could replicate some of the dinners we had, but back here in the USA I think fried chicken, green beans, potato salad and biscuits should do the trick." Sherry was coating the chicken with a secret recipe handed down by her mother. It would set in the covered bowl overnight in the refrigerator.

"You get no argument from me. I never tasted better fried chicken than what you and your mama came up with. You could have had your own chicken chain with that recipe," Jerry said seriously. "Do you want me to dice the potatoes?"

"Yes please, and cover them with water, add a little lemon juice and put them in the 'fridge. The water should keep them from turning dark."

Together they prepared everything for an early start. "By the way m'lady, where are we enjoying this picnic?"

"I heard of a beautiful lake just inside the Tennessee line past Spruce Pine. I thought a nice drive through the mountains to see them awakening from winter would be nice. Maybe see some wild life and sit by the lake and watch the boats and fishermen as we enjoy a picnic."

"Wildlife, that sounds good to me," said Jerry as he took his love into his arms. "If we are through in here let's see if we can look for that wildlife starting tonight."

"I'll tell you what Dr. Wiley, you start the hot tub, I will make lemonade and we will see what develops. Does that fit your schedule?" Sherry said smiling with one of her new winks!

"Your humble servant is off to the hot tub. That fits my schedule to a 'T'," he said as he got one last kiss and headed out to start a beautiful night. All was good in their world, here in Hawthorne.

This proves that a city boy can find real happiness in a small town, and solid love from a small town girl — even if she is a doctor.

CHAPTER 2

Early the next morning along with cooking, Sherry had printed a trip map and directions that showed turning north out of Gastonia. They would simply follow highway 321 all the way. The house smelled great. The fried chicken and coffee smelled good to Jerry. Whistling as he donned some jeans and walking shoes, and then joined his wife in the kitchen.

"Okay sweetheart, what is my assignment?"

"You can start loading the food that is on the bar into the ice chests while the chicken drains a few more minutes. I am going to get dressed. You can just lay the chicken on this towel in the bowl and pack it too. By the way I have already eaten. Yours is beside your coffee. It is egg and livermush," Sherry said as she checked the stove to make sure all the burners were off.

Jerry smiled at the name of the North Carolina food — livermush. He compared it to the scrapple he was used to eating in Pennsylvania and he was acquiring a taste for it. It seemed less greasy than scrapple. Biting into the combination biscuit he was admiring his wife's ability to make a complicated task seem so simple.

Sherry was back just as Jerry was finishing his biscuit. While he ate he had prepared two black coffees to go. "Ready to load up?" she asked.

"As Ed would say, has a cat got a climbing gear?" Jerry smiled, as he thought of Ed, a dear friend, "Let's get to it."

Within minutes they were on the road. The drive is a beautiful one. North of Gastonia, past Gaston College they ran into some beautiful rolling hills like North Central Missouri. Past Hickory they started to see and feel mountains and through Lenoir the road started climbing to Blowing Rock.

At Blowing Rock, Jerry chose to drive into the small 'down town' instead of the bypass. Blowing Rock is a beautiful town. It is the 'Mitford' of author Jan Karon's hit series. Both Jerry and Sherry had reveled in the adventures of Father Tim of Mitford. Blowing Rock is an old town with some fantastic views. They were both ready after an hour and a half of riding to stroll the town park and use the facilities.

Back in the car they headed to Boone, home of Appalachian State University. It is a beautiful college, mountain town. Then they went through town toward the Tennessee state line. As they neared the state line Jerry suddenly stopped the car. After making sure no one was close behind, he made a reverse turn and headed back.

"What's wrong honey?" Sherry asked.

"I hope he is still there. You've got to see this deer," Jerry said excitedly.

As he pulled over to the side, the magnificent animal was still there, standing about seventy five yards off the road. "That is no deer. That dude is a giant elk. I read that they were reintroducing them to the Smoky Mountains but this is far afield. Isn't he beautiful?" Sherry agreed as they sat admiring the elk.

Then as if on cue he looked over at them, sprang off the high ground into the brush, and was gone. "Sweetheart, I am so glad we took this drive. I haven't seen an elk since visiting Yellowstone. They are beautiful creatures."

Realizing the show was over, they turned around and continued their day trip. They crossed the state line and it wasn't long until beautiful Lake Watauga came into sight. "I am not sure where the picnic area is, but it will probably be visible. Pull off when you see a good place," said Sherry.

The picnic area and restrooms were obvious and Jerry found a very good view of the lake. They sat in the car just relaxing and looking. Sherry snuggled over as close as she could and said, "Now this is nice, the mountains, a lake and a day out with the man of my dreams."

After a few minutes of relaxing they stepped outside to a nice warm spring day. It was a little warmer than either had expected. "Let's claim this table with a table cloth and walk around a little," said Jerry, "I want to stretch my legs.

In a few minutes they were walking toward the lake, speaking to a few visitors as they passed tables. There were even a few sun bathers and boat watchers. There was no one fishing from the banks, but a couple of boats were out. Of course one Skidoo, the toy of choice on the water, was out.

On around the water's edge where there was no action, they saw a line of turtles on a log soaking up the sun. One had a bird on its back picking at something on its huge shell. They watched for a minute then turned back toward their table.

"Those guys have the right idea,"

"Which guys?" queried Sherry.

"The two with the back packs. They must be headed into the mountains for the weekend. That is always fun, roughing it for a couple of days. Lots of business men do it just to unwind."

As the two hikers disappeared in the distance, Sherry said thoughtfully, "That might be fun. Do they cook or take sandwiches?"

Jerry smiled, "To be honest, the only time I carried a pack I was working on some CIA operation. We carried the same food to eat as the military. At first it was C-rations, then it was called MRE's. MRE's were prepared food that needed some heating. Some of it was actually pretty good. I don't know how these guys handle their food. They might eat pork and beans. I love 'em," explained Jerry.

Soon they were back at the table unloading and spreading a meal much more than they would eat. Sherry set a beautiful table, even in the woods. "Looks and smells great honey," Jerry said complimenting his wife, "This," indicating the table, "the great outdoors and the feeling of freedom is enough to thank God for."

"Then let's pray," They both bowed and Sherry blessed the food. The food was still very warm, just right for a picnic. Sherry dished portions onto the plates while Jerry fixed their tea. They talked as they ate. Their conversations for the past few months had seemed to angle back to the fantastic vacation they had enjoyed with their friends last year.

"Pardon me," they had been engrossed and did not see the small backpacker close by. "Do you mind if I drop my pack here while I make a visit to the ladies room?"

"I'm sorry we were carried away talking and didn't see you come up. Of course, drop it there. We will be here awhile and will be glad to watch it," answered Jerry.

"Thanks, this is our first pack-off for the day and I don't want to miss a real bathroom," the little lady said as she headed off toward the toilets.

"She is awfully young to be out here. Did you

see how dirty she was?" asked Sherry.

"I guess it is more than a weekend outing."

"Here comes another one," said Sherry as she nodded in the direction the other backpacker had come from.

The dirty guy came closer, but not as close as the lady had. "Excuse me, that is 'Half-Pints' pack I see. Is she off to the latrine?"

"Yes, a lady hiker did drop it off. She didn't leave a name," said Jerry smiling.

"I'm 'Freight Train' by the way, Me 'n Half Pint are married and hiking together, sort of a honeymoon in the wild. We are out for a while, until my classes in Forestry start in the Fall." He was now looking over their shoulders and said, "Hey babe I was just passing the time of day. You ready to hit it again?"

"Sure, let me get my pack."

"Are you guys out for the weekend?" asked Sherry.

Both hikers laughed, "We are out for a few weekends," said the guy.

"Where are you headed?" asked Jerry.

"We are going to Mt. Katahdin in Maine."

"Is that like the state of Maine?" asked Sherry

bewildered.

"Oh, I'm sorry, you are not aware that the Appalachian Trail passes through here? The trail goes straight across the Watauga Dam," the man informed them.

"Come on over and tell us about it," said Sherry.

"We couldn't do that," said the guy called Freight Train.

" Why is that?" asked Sherry.

"Ma'am, we haven't had a bath in a few days…."

"Seven days, Freight!" Broke in Half Pint, "What he is saying is we stink!"

"Please, come to the table and join us. I can tell my wife is itching to hear this story. I have given her some wild ones, but I think you guys are gonna top mine. Please, come on over and join us. We are not that fragile."

After a few minutes both packs were off and Sherry was fixing them a plate, and Jerry was getting tea. "Now tell us about it," coaxed Sherry.

"Well, to start with, I am Pete Thomas and

this is my wife Linda. We both plan to be Forest Rangers eventually so we thought this would be good training for us. Every hiker on the AT adopts or is given a trail name. I have always called Linda 'Half Pint' because she was born in DeSmit, South Dakota the home of the 'Little House On The Prairie'. She in turn called me Freight Train because at times I am a little fast for her," he said smiling.

"Forgive our manners, this food is delicious. We haven't eaten real food since 'Mountain Mama's Hostel' just this side of the Smoky's," said Linda.

"What do you eat when you are out in the woods? My husband and I were just talking about that a few minutes ago when we noticed two more backpackers pass this way." asked Sherry.

"Those two were 'River Rat' and 'Tonto'. We have been passing and being passed for the last fifty miles. But to our food, we like dried fruit for breakfast and a pack of cheese crackers for our lunch and we have settled to ramen noodles in the evening. We like them and it is our only hot meal of the day. They are easy to fix and most of all they are very light to carry," answered Linda with a smile.

The conversation went on for almost an hour. Sherry was fascinated that folks could even attempt to hike over two thousand miles. All the information that Freight Train and Half Pint had shared was too much to digest at one time. Her mind was going a mile a minute.

"We want to thank you for the meal. It was fantastic, but we have to head on up the trail. There is a shelter near here. We will stop and read the shelter log book, relax a little and then try to get five or six more miles in after that before making camp," said Freight Train.

Goodbyes were said, and ignoring the smell, Sherry had to hug Half Pint. Sherry and Jerry stood watching as the two hikers headed on over the Watauga Lake Dam. As they left Half Pint had said, "You guys are Trail Angels. We have met some of the best people while hiking. We are learning more and more that there are some wonderful people in the world. To tell the truth I was becoming cynical."

The hikers had explained that folks all along the AT who help the hikers are referred to as

'Trail Angels'. Some place jugs of fresh water at trail crossings, others leave fruit. In Sherry's mind, a whole new world was beginning to grow. They stayed at the park a few more hours than they had planned just to see if more hikers passed their way.

They met three more hikers. 'Boats' from New Orleans, Papa Smurf from Virginia and Sir Richard from England all of them planning a thru-hike. It was very obvious that all of the backpackers were 'in love' with 'THE TRAIL'. Sherry and Jerry were being introduced to another 'community'. People who follow the blaze. The blaze is a two inch by six inch white marker painted on trees, rocks and roads to indicate the famous Appalachian Trail. Hardy folk, all with a different reason for their hike, but all in love with this two thousand mile foot path.

They cleaned up their scraps, and repacked the car. Then they sat as the sun set in the mountains thinking of the hundreds of backpackers spread from Georgia to Maine, thinking of terms they had heard for the first time today: NOBOs (North bounders), SOBOs (South bounders), through hikers, section hikers, shelters, blue blazing and slack packing.

Reaching across the table Sherry took Jerry's hand, "We can do it!"

"Do what, sweetheart?"

"Hike the Appalachian Trail."

"WHAT?"

"We can do some studying and hike this trail."

"Sherry, I have truly enjoyed the day and meeting these guys. I will admit the thought gets my blood to moving, but we are just a little older than these kids we met today. But we can talk about it. Now let's head home. We are going to get in late. We might just have to stop at a motel," Jerry said with a wink.

'WE can hike this trail,' thought Sherry as they headed back to Mount Bell.

Chapter 3

It was surprising how both Sherry and Jerry started thinking intently about the Appalachian Trail. Researching and reading everything they could about the trail. The one book they could not put down was a novel, 'A Walk in The Woods' by Bill Bryson. It is funny and serious but it whetted their appetite for more.

Jerry was reading for information. Sherry was reading to see if her desire to hike could be changed to a physical accomplishment. Many things that she ran across, she would go to Jerry for clarification, such as water purification and stoves. The more she learned the more she felt like she and Jerry could do it. The more she talked the more Jerry tried to discourage her. He really felt like they would be pushing the envelope at their age.

Finally, after a week, Jerry decided to humor his wife. Sherry was staring intently at her lap top where she had a state by state map of the trail. She realized Jerry was standing behind her. When he was sure she knew he was there he said, "Why don't we get some backpacking gear and do a couple nights on the AT. That will give us an idea if we can even hack it."

"Oh Jerry, could we? You really don't

mind?"

"Yes we can and no I do not mind because I would love to get you in a tent!" He winked and smiled.

She stood up, gave him one of her new winks and said, "Okay dude, I am not sure if I can do it, but I really do want to try. I figure you can protect me from bears and boogers, can't you?"

"I will be at your service my queen. Along with being your protector, I will also show you my expertise in boiling water."

"We need a couple things," reflected Jerry, "One is to shop for the basics for back-packing and two is to find a good place to give it a try. I have an idea on that later. I know you have been following some hiker journals. Why not put out a query about the best place to give the AT a try. How does that sound?"

"Sounds good to me. I will get right on the search for a spot for our trial run. Meanwhile, you pick the shopping places and we will go anytime you are ready," said Sherry as she turned back to her laptop.

Jerry did a search for back packing gear. To his surprise there were a couple places in Gastonia. One was the Sports Authority. It was within a few miles. On his computer he went to the notebook page and started making a list of what they would need. On the screen he saw the list growing:

tent	backpacks	sleeping bags
canteens	flash lights	extra batteries
stove/fuel	bug spray	light clothes
rain gear	matches pot	spoons
first aid supplies	rope	whistle
toilet paper	cat hole scoop	knife
camera	hat	boots

Rain gear? He thought, 'maybe we will pick a couple days with a great forecast for the trial. Water is important but do we need a purifier hiking in the mountains or is that just a sales pitch?'

Jerry had lots of questions, not that he cared about the cost of the supplies but there was no need to purchase something they would not use.

What he needed to do was get the basic essentials. He did not think this would ever go from a seed to complete fruition or would it? As he looked over at Sherry, sitting at the bar intently studying something on her laptop, he thought, she just might have us out there fighting the bugs and mosquitoes for months.

"Got it!" he heard Sherry yell out in triumph.

"Got what, excited lady?" said Jerry as he got up and walked over to the bar.

"Nature Boy says the ideal place is near Standing Indian, in western North Carolina near Franklin. There is a National Park there."

"Sounds good, what makes it a great place for a trial?"

Sherry continued excitedly, "He said the beauty of the area is we will not need a trail shuttle. We can start and go for a couple days and be right back a half mile or so from where we started. It is like a loop thru some beautiful country. I'm calling it up on the map. He says some hikers Blue Blaze it but they miss some great trail."

"Now, what was it exactly that Half Pint said about Blue Blazing?" asked Jerry.

"Well as we know now the AT is marked by a white blaze. The side trails into towns or some special places of interest are marked by 'blue blazes'. She said sometimes the blue blazes cut off part of the AT and some hikers in a rush will follow the blue to save time," Sherry reminded him.

"Yeah, I remember now. That's cheating in many hiker's eyes."

Sherry continued, "You got it. He says when you turn off US64 toward Standing Indian you follow the road until you see the sign to the camp ground. It is a right turn and not far in you will see a small parking area with a picnic table off in the distance. You can park there. Here we have a choice. We can make a southbound trip for 12 miles or walk on down the road, thru the campground, and take the blue blaze up to the AT, then make a northbound trek of 12 miles practically back to the car. It sounds ideal to me."

"I agree, sounds like a winner. So tomorrow we will shop for some backpacking gear. Then check some maps, times and weather and give it a shot! We aren't too old for a little adventure, are we sweet cake?"

"No, we are not, and I am getting all excited. Maybe it is a good time to head for bed again."

"Well Romeo, let's do the hot tub and lemonade thing and then go to bed and sleep on it."

"At times Juliet, you are a kill joy, but I still love you! Let's do it."

****

The next morning it was oatmeal and toast with coffee on the front porch to see the neighbors heading out to work. After the second cup and lots of talk about the world's longest maintained foot path, the AT, they were ready to go shopping.

Armed with the list they entered Sports Authority. They walked around first just looking at the vast array of hiking and camping supplies.

"Good morning folks. What can I interest you in today. I am Seth."

"Well Seth we old folks are looking for enough backpacking gear for a one or two day back packing trip. By the way Seth, are you a hiker by chance?"

"Yes sir, I have hiked our local attraction, Crowder's Mountain. I did make it three hundred miles on the Appalachian Trail between high school and college, but my knee gave out in Virginia. I hated to give it up. My partner made it all the way."

"Then you are the man. My girl here thinks she might want to hike the AT. Our idea is to give it a try for a couple days to see if we are in shape enough to make it," said Jerry.

"Let's walk over to the tents," Seth leading the way, "Are you going to practice on the AT or somewhere else?"

Sherry said, "The Standing Indian area was suggested by Nature Boy."

"You are kidding, you read Nature Boy's Journal?" asked Seth excitedly.

"I just started reading it. He is funny and yes he is the one who suggested Standing Indian," answered Sherry.

"Here are the tents. Are you going to use one or two tents? While you are thinking, I have got to tell you NB is one cool dude. We hiked with him through the Smoky's on his second thru-hike, then he left us in the dust."

Jerry said, "I like to be close to my girl, so it will be one tent."

The back and forth went on and they finally decided on the lightest two man tent at less than four pounds.

Sherry liked the light external frame pack while Jerry preferred the internal frame. The stove was decided to be a gas canister type, the most simple to operate, but heavier. The pot was simple, and it included spoons with a top that could serve as a frying pan if desired.

Seth was a wealth of knowledge, along with

some stories of the AT. "By the way, if you talk with Nature Boy tell him 'Tar Heel' said hello and thanks again for the vitamin I."

"Seth, my wife and I are both doctors. We have never prescribed vitamin I," Jerry laughed.

"Hey Doc, it's a trail thing. Vitamin I is Ibuprofen. We probably over did it, but out in the woods it seems the right thing to do if your knee or ankle is dragging."

"Point well taken, now about water purifiers?"

Seth suggested they carry plenty of drinking water and also use the purification pills in the water you use for cooking. If you need more for the short run use the tablets. They do give the water a little taste, but you won't be out long. Then if you plan to challenge the trail, come back and get the hand pump purifier. It is great."

The suggestion was to always stay less than 25% of your body weight for your pack. It takes some planning but you do not want to hurt yourself, Seth had said. They took his suggestions on the 32 degree sleeping bags. They are lighter and seldom on the AT will you encounter freezing temps, although some have, when they started in February or ended at Katahdin in November.

"I figure we will check for good weather and not need to worry about rain gear," Jerry commented when Seth got to that.

"Doctor, you are probably right, but on my short hike, I found you could not predict the mountain weather. Better at least get a couple light ponchos," was Seth's suggestion, which they heeded.

After a little more conversation about the AT, Jerry and Sherry continued to shop for the smaller items. Jerry also got a Swiss Knife. His was in Pennsylvania.

Seth said as they headed for the clothes, "There is a saying on the trail, 'cotton is rotten', heed it. You will get wet and want the clothes to dry soonest, cotton won't! Also, about Standing Indian, NB is right. It is beautiful country, a little tough stuff and a lot of sweet walk. I hope you decide to do the whole thing. Please let me know how it comes out."

They were acting like two kids. Sherry saw a trail shower. "This looks interesting, but it's four pounds, that is too heavy, right?" she asked. Jerry smiled thinking, 'Maybe we are getting too serious about this trip.' With two carts full they headed for the checkout counter.

Sherry looked seriously at Jerry, "We must carry everything here plus more, right?"

"Seems to be the only way, unless we get a burro, but they aren't allowed on the trail," laughed Jerry.

Everything was loaded in the car and they headed home. They were both excited to get home and start putting the stuff together and, last of all, get on the scales.

They discussed the food to carry and both thought instant oatmeal sounded good, along with some dried fruit. The candy and cracker snack mid-day and ramen noodles to end the day. They were both getting into this idea. It could be fun, even for old folks.

Chapter 4

On the way home from the outfitters they had stopped for some groceries they would carry on the trail. Sherry liked the very small chocolate candies so they bought a variety pack of the small individually wrapped candy bars. They agreed that would be their sweet treats a couple times a day.

With everything spread over the living room floor they started to divide the gear into two stacks. Seth had suggested Jerry carry the food and the lion's share of the water. For the first trip they were going to have three sixteen ounce water bottles. Two on the pack and one on their belt or pack straps available to sip on as they hiked.

The bathroom scale was in the living room

now as they donned the packs. Jerry was registering 45 pounds and Sherry 37 pounds. They both seemed to be comfortable with the weight, but the packs did not feel comfortable.

The instructions for adjusting the packs were confusing. Not knowing which strap was being referred to in the dialog, they were constantly going back to the pictures for ID. After an hour they were both disgusted at trying to follow the detailed instructions and put them aside.

They had much better luck going by the feel of the pack. The process was feeling better. Both of them had selected a sort of 'belly' pack that has a water bottle holster and a zip up section for notes, maps and miscellaneous stuff. Sherry selected a couple bite size chocolate bars and a pack of peanut butter crackers. Jerry, smiling broadly, copied her! "I knew you could not resist a chocolate snack," she said grinning.

At that, jerry added a small box of raisins. Sherry followed, "I like raisins too Dr. Wiley!"

"Let's take a walk around the common area,"

Jerry suggested.

"No way, people will see us and think we are crazy!"

"Well?... Aren't we?"

"Okay you silver tongued devil, let's go," Sherry said as she picked up a couch pillow to act like she was going to keep her face covered. They both burst out laughing.

"See, we are crazy old people," Jerry said as he held the door for her to exit.

If anyone was watching it was from inside. No one was out in the common area and they made a swing down the hill and back up. After a hundred yards, both of them needed to adjust the shoulder straps. It took only a couple minutes and they both felt comfortable. Going back up the hill they again stopped for another adjustment. "I cannot believe they make a pack so complicated," stated Sherry.

"I agree and I am surprised. All the packs I have carried must have been pre-adjusted, but wait — I was younger," Jerry said with a big smile, "Carry on my leader."

Back in the living room, the packs were dropped. "What do you really think Jerry?"

"Oh, we can muddle thru a couple days. We will definitely learn something. You look good with a pack lady; you ask what do I think? — methinks we can definitely do twelve to twenty miles in a couple days."

Sherry hugged him tight, "I think so too, darling. When are we going?"

"I say you get us a reservation in a motel near to Standing Indian, probably in Franklin. We can spend Wednesday night there and start our maiden hike Thursday morning. With any luck we will be back in Mount Bell by Saturday night, and we can pray for healing Sunday in church," Jerry said showing another big smile.

They cleared up all the wrappings and bags for disposal. Sherry carefully held onto the warranties and receipts to file them. Jerry knew she would have an account of all expenses for her test run. He also knew if they were to actually attempt to hike the AT she would also have a journal. He was proud of his wife. He knew his conservative father, if he were alive, would also approve highly of this lady he had chosen late in life.

Jerry had never been much on nostalgia. He had been a 'here and now' person. But lately he had thought of his father and mother. They had always wanted grandchildren but he was too wrapped up in goals and ideal aims to look for love and marriage. He had been afraid they would have squelched his innovativeness. 'Little did I know there was a mate like Sherry who would have added to my dreams. For a smart fellow, Jerry, you were very narrow minded,' he thought.

"Grandchildren" he said to himself he thought, "Tuck, J Leon, Buddy and Sticky would have been good enough for dad, had he known them."

"What was that?" Sherry asked.

"Oh, just talking to myself. I was thinking,

mama had always wanted grandkids. She and dad would have loved my boys even if they are not flesh and blood."

"Anyone would love that pack. So I am sure they would have."

While Jerry was day dreaming, Sherry had made reservations and the trip was set.

****

Wednesday they were in good spirits as they had loaded the car. Doctors are methodic and exact as a rule. The doctors Jerry and Sherry were no different. They had checked and rechecked their lists. They covered many subjects on the ride up. Of course Sherry had talked to her high school classmates, telling them their plans.

"Evelyn could not believe we were going to do this. She was sure this was not in their plans. She said they had fought enough bugs and mosquitoes out on the farm, but wished us luck."

"I talked to Tuck and he laughed. Couldn't wait to call our other 'sons'," Jerry said.

The motel was nice, but neither slept too

well, anticipating the next day's journey. The motel had a small restaurant. They ate a good breakfast and headed for Standing Indian.

After turning off US 64 and driving a piece Sherry said, "Stop Jerry." There was no traffic so Jerry pulled over to the side, "Back up to that sign."

They both laughed, the sign read 'Welcome to the Rainbow Springs Hostel, Home of the World's Best Chili'. The laughing was because this Hostel and the Chili was mentioned in the book, 'A Walk in the Woods'. "Nature Boy didn't mention this. We will have to stop on the way back. Now continue Sir Jerry."

The area was just as Nature Boy had described it. They found the parking spot. There was one car there already. They had decided to walk the road thru the campground and go up to the AT. At the campground they asked a ranger where the Blue Blaze trail to the AT was.

"There are two trails. One is a little steep. The other is best and it runs beside the creek. Good luck, lots of hikers this year."

They continued to walk. After about twenty minutes Jerry said, "We must have missed the blazes, let's back track." Starting back they met one of the campers and he pointed out the trail head. They weren't far past it.

Jerry had to admit, the trail was tough but Sherry hung in there. But after climbing about thirty minutes they came to a more level grassy spot. "Pack off time," Jerry announced with a little disgust in his voice. They both lay on the grass with their heads on the packs. Sherry still had not spoken. "Sweetheart," Jerry continued, "We have done some stupid things in our short marriage, but this may take the cake." He was tired and Sherry was about in tears.

"Honey, we have just gotten started, we must have taken the wrong Blue Blaze trail, I still believe we can do it," Sherry said with a little reproof in her voice.

"You are right darling, I'm sorry. I guess I am frustrated because this is not what I was picturing. Of course we can do it."

After the break, some water and a chocolate snack they renewed their climb. It actually got easier and in fifteen minutes they came to a well-worn path. Looking left, they saw their first white blaze. "We made it," exclaimed Sherry and hugged Jerry as well as she could with their packs on. She continued, "Okay my man, lead on."

The walk was much easier and they both began to relax. After walking about a half mile they came to a sign announcing the 'Standing Indian Shelter'. "Let's walk over and check it out said Sherry. I want to read a Shelter Log, it will be my first."

The Shelter was not far off the trail and there was one hiker already there. As they approached she stood, "Hello, I'm Madam Little, just stopped for a snack. I haven't seen you guys before. You guys must be SOBO's. What do they call you?"

"We just walked onto the trail a little while ago. We are really North Bound but not for far. This is sort of a test to see if we can backpack, at my husband's age," Sherry laughed.

"Shoot yeah you can, nothing to it. This is great for your mind and health too. I am here getting psyched up for my senior year in nursing. I plan to go all the way to Katahdin. I figured if I don't do it now, I'd be old before I got the time off, no offense."

"No offense taken because you are right, the medical profession is pretty demanding. So how far have you hiked?"

"Oh I just started, about a hundred miles I think. This has been fun, but I need to make some miles. Best of luck to you guys. Maybe I will see you up the trail somewhere." They all passed a few more words and Madam Little was off.

Sherry and Jerry read some in the Shelter Log. Everyone was upbeat in their entries. The front of the log gave directions to the privy and water supply. After looking around, they headed north.

It was beautiful and quiet. No road noise and

just a cool mountain breeze. They did hit a few rocks to climb over, but overall it was a great foot path. They hiked about two hours and started looking for a good place for a pack off. They had not bought boots for the short trial. Their walking shoes were doing quite well for them. They both spotted a carved direction sign that read, Good View. Just a few yards out was a nice spot to relax and yes the view of the valley below was fantastic.

"Look Jerry," Sherry was pointing to a hawk soaring below them, "I never thought I would be walking above the birds." Out came the crackers and water jugs. It was an amazing thirty minute break. The beauty was overwhelming.

"I must tell you Mrs. Wiley, if all we do is take in some beautiful views, this effort will be worth it. You have chosen well lady." Jerry said as they suited back up to continue their walk.

Enjoying their own thoughts, they continued to walk for a couple more hours. They had done some ups and downs but nothing like the Blue

Blaze introduction trail. This area was really like a walk in a park. "Let's start looking for a place for a camp site and stop for the day. It's about five o'clock," Jerry suggested. They were on a downhill walk now. He was hoping for a flat spot for their tent at the bottom.

"There," pointed Sherry, "It looks like a lot of folk have stopped here beside this stream."

It was a perfect site, and it was easy to see it had been used, but the area was clean, no litter. They were to learn that AT Hikers, as a rule, really cared about the environment.

The camp set up was by the book. Everything worked as planned. So far they hadn't noticed anything missing. Jerry boiled the water and fixed the ramen noodles. He split the meal, Sherry was able to eat out of the lid, but they decided they would need something better. Sherry was ready with the note pad. As they finished, another hiker stopped and asked if they minded him pitching his tent near them. Of course there was no objection. In a little while the neighbor was set up and threw a rope across a limb nearby and pulled his pack to about ten feet off the ground.

Jerry made a small camp fire and they all sat around talking. Jerry learned the practice of hanging the packs was to keep from losing them to animals. So he hung their packs.

They were up the next morning, broke camp, ate, and did the morning rituals. Their neighbor was up and gone before they arose.

The trail did get a little tougher. They walked a 50 yard rock ledge that jutted out about twelve inches from an inclining rock wall. It looked more dangerous than it was. The hiker's weight pulled him to the wall instead of over into the gorge. Jerry's only advice was, "Do not look over the edge; just place your feet on the ledge." By noon they were passing a Forest Service Fire Tower on top of a mountain.

The hike had gone well with several adjustments to the shoulder straps of the packs until they were riding well. The packs had also been repacked to reach things needed. The big adjustment for Sherry was digging the cat-hole for her daily trip to the toilet. They had not checked the privy at the Shelter atop Standing Indian and would not encounter another shelter before reaching the car.

The rest of the hike was just enjoyable, no problems and no tough spots. That area was just a good walk. The advice from Nature Boy had been good. It had been nearly two full days and other than a bad start, everything went well. Once in the car and headed out, Sherry decided not to stop by the hostel with the best chili. She wanted a bath. The two were tired but happy campers when they stopped back at the same motel for the night.

After a bath and a good country dinner they fell into bed. Wrapped in each other's arms Sherry said, "Sweetheart I really do appreciate you humoring me in the back packing idea. I really was not sure if I could do this or if I would enjoy it, but I did it. Now the big question, when can we start toward Mount Katahdin?"

This caught Jerry off guard. He had thought she was going to say the opposite, "Well, first of all, are you pulling my leg, or are you serious?"

"I am serious."

"Then sweetheart, when we get home we will check on maps, check the timing and head out as soon as possible."

"You are the best …"

Jerry started to answer his wife, and turned over to find Sherry was asleep, 'not a 'bear' in the world', he smiled at that thought.

The next day, Sherry's opinion had not changed. The whole trip back was filled with plans.

Chapter 5

By Wednesday of the next week they had Trail Maps, the Appalachian Trail Thru-hikers Companion and an AT Data Book. Jerry had gone back to see Seth at Sports Authority and picked up two light weight bowls that fit in the pot and a water purifier. They had also bought some good socks and boots.

The boot man had made a suggestion, "Slip on some thin nylon socks under the hiking socks and it will help prevent blisters." He had quoted some famous hiker who said he didn't care if the nylon socks got blisters. Jerry gave a good obligatory laugh but it wasn't that funny, at the time.

Sticky, one of their adopted sons, had agreed to check on the mail and keep it boxed for them. They stopped the delivery of the Gaston Gazette. All their utility and insurance bills were drafted. With everything taken care of, they left on Thursday morning. The first stop was the local Hardees for one last biscuit and a short visit with Sherry's old high school mates.

There were lots of jokes about snakes, bears and senior sex on the trail. Ed couldn't miss one about Jerry being the cook and burning the water. None of their friends wanted to join them on the trail. So with a cup of coffee to go, Sherry and Jerry pointed the car for I 85 South towards

Amicalola Falls State Park in Georgia. Springer Mountain, in the park, was the southern terminus of the Appalachian Trail.

"Jerry you are such a sport to indulge me in this silly notion of walking over two thousand miles." Sherry said.

"Honey, I am probably as hyped up about this as you are. With the CIA I was never in the woods just for the fun of it. Come to think of it they never sent a lady with me either. I think I can get to liking this," he said with a wink.

They drove into the state park to look around. The Ranger said to save time they could register now since it was late.   They did and the packs were weighed for the record. Then they headed for Ellijay, a small town nearby. Sherry had the address of an AT shuttle driver who would also store the car for a fee. Betty was a cheerful lady. She suggested they overnight at a local motel. They parked their car took everything they had for the hike and put it all in Betty's van.

She drove them to the motel. She would pick

them up at McDonalds at six in the morning. Jerry and Sherry could not help but notice that every door they saw in Ellijay had a baggie, half filled with water, hanging at the door. It was curious.

It was Friday morning. They had finished their biscuit and coffee when Betty drove up. She had her dog Charlie in the front seat with her. On the way to the trail head Sherry asked about the water baggies. "We have a terrible fly problem this time of the year. For some reason, it keeps most of the flies from entering the door when it is open."

Remembering the incident at Standing Indian getting up to the trail, Jerry had arranged with Betty to take them directly to the AT trail head atop Springer Mountain. A forest service road crossed the trail about a half mile after the actual trail head. Just before the destination Charlie barked. He was barking at a black bear that had just crossed the road. Jerry felt Sherry draw up a little, but she said nothing.

Betty dropped them off at the AT. Jerry had already paid the freight. They had decided to walk back down to the trail head and start from there. Sherry wanted to do every mile. They met several hikers who had climbed Springer Mountain and stayed at the beginning shelter overnight.

They read the plaques at the trail head. The trail up from Amicalola Falls State Park is not part of the AT. They reveled in the idea of the thousands who would start this trek and they were going to be part of it. They hugged, kissed and looked at each other and smiled, "Let's hit it man," Sherry said, giving one of her winks.

They started the trek they hoped would end up in Maine. Jerry had done the math and they had timed themselves. They could walk at about three miles an hour. He had announced, "We have time to do the whole trail, barring any injuries. We should easily be able to do sixteen miles a day. We should finish in October.

They were in a world of their own. Each with

thoughts and plans, they began to observe nature. About an hour into the hike, there were scattered rain drops. Neither deemed it enough to stop and dig out the ponchos. As they continued to walk, they came to the Stover Creek Shelter on the left. They immediately turned in for shelter from the rain. There were several hikers just resting.

They passed the time of day and learned trail names and plans. Everyone planned a thru-hike except 'Tinker', who was a section hiker. He was going to Standing Indian where his wife was going to meet him. It was too early in the day for anyone to plan to over-night here. In just a few minutes the little shower let up and everyone was gone. Sherry and Jerry were the last to leave. Sherry hung back to glance at the shelter log. The others had been reading it and she did not get a chance until they left.

Back on the trail the sun was back out and as they walked Jerry thought of Seth's warning, 'you cannot predict mountain weather.'

Alone with their thoughts the trail almost
seemed level to them. For another hour the trail
started down, pretty steadily, in reference to how
it had been down and up the Georgia Mountains.
They learned that Georgia Mountains were not
high or steep enough for switchbacks (zig-zags)
but basically a straight trail down and back up a
mountain.

Jerry frowned to himself. This was already
wearing on him. They had not gone ten miles
and it was about time to stop for the night. As he
was thinking, Sherry, who was ahead of him,
followed a path off to the right of the trail, a sign
had read 'Vista'. They dropped their packs and
sat on the smooth rocks. The view was breath
taking. They sat, absorbing the gorgeous
mountains and valleys as far as they could see. As
they pulled on the water bottles there were no
words, but they both seemed to think, this is
what it is about. Soon they again hit the trail.
Now they were looking for a good place to pitch
the tent.

After another down they spotted a very good spot to camp. They were tired. The ground cloth first then the tent. Sherry said, "I will be inside for a few minutes," and climbed into the tent carrying her belly back. As a lady will, she had found a way to take a bath, or close, using the 'wet-wipes'.

While sherry took care of business Jerry fixed a spot to cook supper. Then he cleared a spot for a camp fire and gathered some wood. He busied himself around the camp sight. Throwing his rope over a limb to be ready to lift the packs when they turned in.

As promised, Sherry was out of the tent, "Ah, I feel a hundred percent better. What can I do?"

"You can gather a little more firewood and put it on the fire. I started it with some pine cones and needles. An easy one tonight."

"Jerry, I hear a noise," said Sherry in almost a whisper.

"Yeah, I thought I heard something earlier. What direction do you think it is?"

Sherry pointed past a dead tree and Jerry walked over to take a look. "Hey baby, it's a bear, come look." Sherry saw only black ears and that was enough. Back to the fire for her.

Jerry walked over with an armful of wood, "It's not a big one honey, I don't see a problem. Let's eat supper."

He divided the ramen noodles into the new bowls and they sat on the ground quietly eating. Then Jerry broke the silence, "I hear they will not come close to a fire. We will build a good fire before we turn in. But first honey, are you going to be all right?"

"Yeah, I think so. I didn't read of anyone being mauled on the trail, of course I don't want to be the first," she said laughing.
After brushing her teeth Sherry climbed in the tent.

Jerry continued to gather wood. After about fifteen minutes he unzipped the tent to ask if his wife was still okay, and she was fast asleep. He smiled and zipped the tent, walked over to the fire and pulled the rocks closer to the embers to protect the fire from spreading. Then he too was glad to spend the night in his comfortable sleeping bag.

They awoke about the same time. It was light outside. Jerry climbed out to go relieve himself. The mountain air was crisp and woke him up fast. Immediately he lowered the packs and retrieved the stove and oatmeal. Within minutes he had the stove going to boil water for the oatmeal.

After breakfast, he took the time to show Sherry how to use sand to clean her utensils. They rinsed them with water. They were on the trail within thirty minutes. The morning was beautiful. Problem was they were starting at the bottom of a mountain. So there was a morning climb. It wasn't long until they passed the Hawk Mountain Shelter and did not stop. They were again engrossed in their own thoughts while observing nature and the sights provided. Some of these sights they would never see the likes while driving a car.

It was fun seeing the flowers blooming and black berry bushes covered with blooms and some green berries. Then just after a long down run they came to a beautiful water fall. They only observed the beauty. It was a picture of the word 'peaceful'. A hiker had hung his hammock so the falls were just beyond and centered. Jerry thinking, that is a picture, snapped his second shot. They stood there for only a minute before heading on up the trail.

They topped the next mountain and started down. About mid-morning when Sherry called for a pack off break. Time for a bite size candy bar and some water. They had stopped on a narrow spot in the trail. It was sided by grass on an uphill swing. They just lay back in the lush grass.

They were quietly lying there when all of a sudden a guy coming from the north threw his pack beside them, and collapsed in the grass, "I have been looking for just this spot. I'm glad you found it for me," he laughed. "I'm 'The Pilgrim," who be you old folk?"

"We are Jerry and Sherry good to meet you—Old folk? How old are you Pilgrim?"

"Three score and ten friend and you?"

"We are three score and twelve my young friend."

"Jerry and Sherry, huh? Ye look like a couple of Overland Hermits to me."

They learned that the Pilgrim had returned to finish his South bound thru hike. He was on the last leg of his hike. He had dropped out last year because he pulled an Achilles tendon. His story just whetted their appetite. They might actually be able to hike this trail. They enjoyed the Pilgrims story. He had been an accountant for a mining company in Pennsylvania and had just retired. They knew he would finish the trail today or tomorrow.

Getting up and swinging his pack on like a kid, he said, "You will meet Penguin pretty soon. She is a sweet little thing. She is also finishing her hike and she is from South Africa. Last I saw her she was running with a girl from North Carolina. Now, by the way, when you get to my home state, Pennsylvania, eat a half gallon of ice cream and say hello to the rocks for me. Take care," and he was off.

As Jerry and Sherry stood and got ready to go, the Pilgrim's last words were a puzzle to them, 'eat a half gallon of ice cream and say hello to the rocks'. What did he mean?

They headed on north making miles. In about an hour they came to Cooper Gap road and they both knew by the maps it was only twelve miles from Springer Mountain. Jerry knew he had better revise their hiking time. He laughed to himself. Fool yourself once that is okay, adjust and live with it. But try to fool yourself twice, you are in trouble. So I had better think on this tonight.

They had topped a mountain and were walking through a solid tunnel — it seemed a mile long. The tunnel was of beautiful sweet smelling rhododendrons or laurels, neither of them knew the difference yet. They both stopped, the tunnel was wide enough to walk side by side. Ahead was a beautiful site, almost religious. The tunnel had allowed a spear of light to penetrate and it was highlighting a beautiful white flower. It was almost as if nature was saying this beautiful flower's vine is what's sheltering you from the sun. "That is absolutely the most beautiful site I have ever seen," breathed Sherry.

"Amen," was all that Jerry could muster. This was gorgeous.

They started up again, both of them still relishing the sight they had just seen. About half an hour after leaving the beautiful nature's tunnel Jerry said, "It isn't far to the Gooch Mountain Shelter. Let's rest and overnight there, what do you say?"

"Sounds like a winner to me sweetie," lead on.

As their day was waning they came to the shelter. A young man was already there. Jerry got a strange feeling from the guy. One of those, 'I don't think I like this guy, but I don't know why,' feelings. Jerry motioned Sherry to stay on the trail and he went forward to talk. In a few minutes Jerry was back, "Let's go on up the trail a piece."

Sherry sensing something was not right did not question but held her questions until out of range of sight or hearing. "What was the problem, Jerry?"

"The young fellow is doing community serviced for a DUI. I have no problem with that, however, he is drunk now. That is not the fault of the AT nor the courts. The young man has a problem and an attitude. I thought it better to be in a tent again tonight." Sherry agreed and they walked on another hour and camped close to Woody Gap. It was another good camp sight, but to Sherry's relief no bear incident.

The shelter incident did not rain on their parade. They had a good evening. Another couple came up just as they were finishing their noodles. They rushed to set up. They were eating cold. They had decided to have p-nut butter and crackers as their evening meals to cut down on the stove weight. They had a great evening around the camp fire. The new couple's trail names were Skyscraper and Condo. He was the head engineer for the new office building in Charlotte, NC. They were only out for a few day section hiking. They had two dogs with packs. The dogs carried their own food and water. Very interesting.

Jerry and Sherry were beginning to realize just how varied the hikers were. They did not feel so out of place. As they zipped up the tent, they snuggled even though both were in sleeping bags. It had been a good day. Jerry smiled to himself, figuring miles on paper is much different than reality. We have covered only about eighteen miles of the trail in two days. He drifted off to sleep following Sherry to dream world. It was Saturday night.

Chapter 6

As they headed out Sunday morning they left the other couple in their tent. They ate only dried fruit for breakfast. It was a beautiful day for a walk. Sherry said, "When you sleep in the valley, it seems you always have a hill to climb the next day."

"We may try something different his evening. Maybe we will camp on the downhill drag of one of these mountains if we find a camping spot." Jerry was in the lead this morning when he saw the animal droppings. He made the announcement, "Poop on the trail." It had become sort of a game and also a warning for the person, if they were following close behind, not to step in it.

Atop the first mountain they stopped to enjoy the view and drop their packs. "I think squirrels are putting rocks in my pack overnight," said Sherry. "I do believe it is getting heavier."

"I'm about to agree. That theory that the

pack gets lighter as you eat, isn't noticeable four ounces at a time," commented Jerry.

"Would you look at that?" Jerry said as he pointed over to the trail. Both the dogs they had met last night were going by on the trail. "That cracks me up. If I didn't know they were with Skyscraper and Condo I would be thinking dogs were thru-hiking." It was a neat sight the dogs alone carrying packs. They sat looking off into the distance.

"This is a day the Lord hath made, let us rejoice and be glad in it," Sherry quoted reverently. They waved at Skyscraper and Condo as they passed. In a few minutes the trail was empty again, like ships passing.

"The ATC has some good information in the books we bought with the maps. I like the Companion best. We are close to Woody Gap, then about 7 miles to the Woods Hole Shelter. Let's try that tonight."

"I think we can do that, but methinks my prince sorta over estimated what this older woman could hike in a day."

"Let me tell you lady, I realized that long before you did. Maybe our stamina will pick up. We are just starting. We didn't work up to this, but I am not the type to go out and hike a few miles a day to get ready. I believe in jumping in and getting the practice and build some miles. Come to think of it, I think my love is the same."

"I was beginning to worry that I was holding you back and that you expected more from this old lady."

"I guess the mind doesn't age like the body, so I was still thinking from a youthful standpoint. But we will work it out. This is just the beginning, speaking of which....." and they put on their packs to head for the next trail happening. That happened to be only a hundred yards because they ran into a wall of fallen tree. A giant oak had come out of the ground, pulling a big dirt ball with it. They had read of the dead falls and wind falls on the trail. The AT is maintained by many hiking clubs. They would get to this one soon, but right now they had to get across it.

"I am going to climb in to the trunk of the tree and see how we can get by, "Jerry said, but before he could start they heard a voice on the other side.

"Is someone over there?" Came the voice.

"Yes" called Jerry, "Do you see a way around the tree?"

"I think so, but let's work our way into the heart of the tree if we can. I will meet you there. Bring your pack if that's possible."

Jerry worked his way to the trunk of the tree, Sherry following. It would be impossible to crawl under. There were too many limbs crushed. But in ten minutes they all had met at the trunk. It was another couple hikers sectioning south. They worked out a system to pass the packs over and soon everyone was over and through the tree, and they had made new friends, 'Pedal and Medal'.

They were laughing as they continued north, "You didn't count on that type delay, did you?"

asked Sherry.

"No ma'am, but I have already figured it in for the future." Jerry stepped up beside her to squeeze her and steal a kiss. Soon they were at Woody Gap, where they noticed jugs of water, with a note stating water for Thru-hikers only, signed your Trail Angel. "What a nice gesture." Jerry said, "See baby, there are angels just like you said."

"You told me I was always right, Dr. Wiley." Sherry said, giving 'the wink'.

They were tired but they did make the Woods Hole Shelter before too late. Another couple of hikers were already there and had their sleeping bags laid on the floor of the shelter. After eating they had time to talk and learned about the 'written and unwritten rules for shelters'. There is always room for one more. In the rain there is room for EVERYONE, if they have to stand. Hang your food from the mice. They are here. Keep it clean for the next hiker. Keep the water source clean and always use the privy when it is available. If no privy is available use the far side of the shelter away from the water source. They smiled when they learned that actually, up in New England, there were snoring and non-snoring shelters. No one else showed up for the night so they had a comfortable night for their first shelter night. They had now made it twenty eight miles in three days. "Not bad for a couple old folk," Sherry said.

The next day they climbed the highest peak on the AT in Georgia, Blood Mountain. At the top of the mountain was an enclosed rock shelter. It even had a door. As they sat, they had a pleasant surprise. Up walked Penguin, the young hiker from South Africa. She had no pack, but was accompanied with a handsome guy. "Ah, Freddie, this is the 'Overland Hermits' I met just before finishing my thru-hike."

Both Sherry and Jerry stood to accept the out stretched hand of Freddie. "Penguin, what are you doing back on the trail?" asked Sherry.

"Ma'am", she said with her South African

accent very apparent, "I am showing Freddie some of the highlights of the Appalachian Trail. He met me at the Southern Terminus, after flying in from South Africa."

They passed some conversation, but it was apparent the youngsters were ready to head back down the trail. After they left Jerry said, "Wow she has some endurance. I would be sitting in a hotel soaking my feet."

"That is the difference in youth and age my dear sir, youth and age," Sherry said, then concluded, "I guess it is official we are the "Overland Hermits".

They hiked on down to Neel's Gap. The trail actually goes right thru the Neel's Gap Outfitters store. Here, the owner called them a shuttle and they headed for a motel, a shower and a bed. What a nice old bed.

They took a shuttle back to the AT the next morning. They restocked and were on the trail by nine AM.

They made it through Hog Pen Gap, about

eleven miles to Low Gap Shelter. They were beat. Ate some noodles and stretched out on the Shelter floor. Both were asleep before nine PM and were the only ones at the shelter for the night.

They were up and wearing their packs by eight AM. They walked along and both were thinking, this is a little tougher than I thought. They were dragging when they made it to Unicoi Gap. There was a shuttle phone number on the bulletin board. Jerry used the cell to call. They had long ago decided to overnight at Unicoi. After all, this was the famous Helen, Georgia crossing. It was also where Mull's Motel was located. They must spend the night there after reading 'A Walk in The Woods'.

Peggy arrived in a van, they talked a few minutes and she drove them to Mull's Motel where they checked in. They had hiked nine miles and they were beat. They both crashed for a nap, then bathed and Sherry relaxed in the tub for an hour. Later, they ate at Kentucky Fried where they had the all-u-can-eat special.

They did walk around Helen awhile and made sure they were stocked up. It felt good leaving the packs in the motel. They planned to sleep late in the morning. Peggy would pick them up at Mull's at eleven AM. Sherry's shoulder straps were cutting into her shoulders, so the next morning, after a relaxing breakfast they went shopping. They found some strips of sponge at a Thrift Store, and a roll of duct tape. Jerry took time to pad both their pack's shoulder straps.

Peggy was at Mulls at exactly eleven and they were soon back on the trail. The Mull's had been a wonderful couple who joked about Bryson's down grading their motel. "We knew it was embellishing to sell books, so who cares. It sure advertised this little motel," Mrs. Mull had said, "He put us on the map."

The driver gave Jerry her card. "If you need me again in the next hundred miles give me a call." As Peggy drove off, a new Cadillac pulled in. A nicely dressed couple got out with a young girl who was dressed for the trail. The man walked over to Jerry. "Hi, my name is Carl Jennings. Are you hiking the AT?"

"Jerry Wiley here, and yes we are hiking north."

"Man, am I glad to see you. Susan has set her mind to hike from here to Maine. Her mama and I are scared stiff, but if you are headed that way I would appreciate it if you kept an eye on her."

"Mr. Jennings, I am sure Susan will do fine. We have met some wonderful young folk on the trail, but we will do what we can."

The Jennings were still parked when the three headed out of sight, lost in the Laurel.

They had gone only a short distance when Susan stopped. "Now folks, I know my daddy said to look after me, but they still do not know I have grown up. I am getting ready for my second year of nursing school. This is my time out. I have always wanted to hike this trail. We only live twenty miles from the crossing. My daddy raises chickens and he watches them grow.

Somehow, he has missed seeing me grow. "

"Yes, your dad did ask me to keep an eye on you. Of course we would only hold you back. You take care and have a good hike."

"By the way, I am 'The Good Nurse' and thanks for understanding." Susan immediately turned and left them in the dust and they were laughing.

"She thinks she is grown enough for the world. Her parents think she is still a kid and they are all wonderfully wrong," Sherry said, with an understanding smile.

"The Mulls' were sure understanding about the treatment Bryson gave them in the book," said Jerry, as they walked. "They show good business sense not to bad mouth him. It is for sure we are not the only ones showing up because of the book. I just wish we had not left our hiking sticks there, but he assured me, when I called back, that they would hold onto them for us."

"These you picked up will do just fine for a

while. They are pretty sturdy," answered Sherry.

As was true for most of the hike, they were both soon off in a world of their own, enjoying the outdoors and the spectacular scenes when they reached the high ground.

Jerry was trying not to complain too much, but the soles of his feet were burning and giving him trouble. He and Sherry were different in their approach to the hike. Where he liked going up, she preferred the down hills. Jerry's problem was his toes hit the end of his boots as they slipped inside going downhill, making his toes sore also.

After walking a couple hours, they stopped and dropped their packs. Out came the water bottles and a pack of cheese crackers. This was a good time on the hike to sit and watch nature. The scene they saw this time was unusual. Within five feet in front of them a small toad jumped past in a hurry. A second later, they knew why. A garden snake, about three feet long, was in hot pursuit. Jerry called out, "Stop" the snake stopped and looked over at them, "I think you just missed supper mister snake," Jerry said, hoping the toad could get away as the snake slowly crawled off.

"Well this short time on the trail has changed me," said Sherry, "I would never have believed I could sit still with a snake that close. But I think you saved the toad's life, honey."

"He might have missed his supper. I am thinking how good the subs in my pack are going to be for supper." In Jerry's pack were two foot long subs they planned to enjoy for supper. No cooking tonight.

Back on the trail for another hour and they found a great place for a campsite. Sherry did her wet wipe bath and Jerry gathered wood. They relaxed and enjoyed some family time, even a little smooching. As they enjoyed the evening several folk stopped by to chat. They got the conditions of the trail ahead and pointed the hikers to a spring not fifty feet off the trail. Before the sun set, they ate their sandwiches. They lay back on the grass and enjoyed the time as the sun set. This was how Sherry had pictured the trail. She was happy.

The morning of the fourth day out of Unicoi Gap they came to the Georgia—North Carolina state line. Of course Jerry set the timer and took their picture in front of the sign. A few miles back they had gone two hundred feet off the trail to the head waters of the Chattahoochee River, a spring. For some inner reason Jerry was overwhelmed. "You know I have never seen an actual head waters before. Strange, before this reaches the low lands it is a river. I have never thought too much about it, but every river must start somewhere."

But here they were at their first state line. Jerry was thinking, this is tougher than I expected. I cannot believe my girl hasn't cried UNCLE. My feet are killing me.

On they plodded, and in a few miles came to a Forest Service road with a sign pointing to 'Standing Indian Campground 3 Miles'. "Honey, if you don't mind, instead of climbing the mountain, let's Blue Blaze and get a camp site and bathe," Sherry said, apologetically.

"Sweetheart, that is music to my ears. My feet are killing me. Lead on," Jerry said.

They stopped once more on a break. "Honey, how do you feel about the hike?" asked Jerry.

"I am enjoying it," said Sherry, "But it is tougher than I thought."

"My feelings exactly," said Jerry thoughtfully. "I have been thinking, maybe we had better drop back and regroup. I will call Peggy and have her pick us up here at Standing Indian and take us back to the car. We need to do some more planning if we are to continue."

"I hate to quit. What will my friends think?"

"They will say, you walked a hundred miles! WOW I could never do that. Seriously how many folk do you know who have backpacked one hundred miles, really?"

"You are right, of course. Let's head to the campground."

The campground was in sight with a small

stream to cross on a log. Jerry mounted the log and started across with Sherry following. Jerry heard a quiet "Oh, Jerry," and he turned to see Sherry falling backwards into the shallow creek. Once she was down she was laughing, and Jerry heard her say, "I think I will just lay here."

They were a sight entering the campground, both soaked and laughing.

Chapter 7

After securing the ride back to Ellijay and retrieving the car they headed back to Mt. Bell. Of course there were phone calls back to the class mates to let them know 'I am coming home with my tail between my legs'. Fact was everyone was glad to know they were coming home.

Before arriving back at Mt. Bell they had plans for next year, better and more logical plans including a few short hikes over the next six months.

Their short adventure was the talk of the get-together at Hardee's. They all enjoyed the stories especially the trail names. Now Sherry and Jerry were known as the Hermits. There was a lot of good natured fun.

At home most of their spare time was spent reading and studying about the Appalachian Trail. Sherry kept hyped up by reading trail journals on the net. Hikers were now headed for Damascus Virginia and what was called 'Trail Days'.

They had settled on their plan of attack next year. It was to start next spring at Fontana Dam and hike south to US 64. They had decided to use an AT shuttle. By parking their car on Route 64 and getting a shuttle driver to take them to Fontana they could hike back to their car. Then they would have the option to quit or drive to Tennessee and park the car. Then hire a shuttle back to Fontana and hike north. They would be attacking the Great Smoky Mountains, a hike of approximately one hundred miles. That sounded exciting to both of them. They loved the Smoky Mountains.

Jerry was a tinker. He had found an alcohol stove design. The weight was less than an ounce and the denatured alcohol fuel would be light. On the back porch he had made two of them and practiced boiling water. He improved the design by forming a shield that was also a pot holder. Sherry was impressed. They were like a couple of kids, having a ball thinking of this adventure ahead.

A few weeks after returning from the trail, Sherry asked, "Honey, do you feel like a little hike?"

"Of course Doctor. What do you have in mind?"

"There are about three miles between where we left the trail at Standing Indian and Highway 64. It should be an easy six miles. We could go up and hike that, then drive around to Fontana and see what the land looks like. What do you say?"

"Sounds good. We could carry a light day pack with a snack and some water. When do you want to do it?" asked Jerry.

Pausing and smiling her 'smile', she said, "How about in the morning?"

"You are on lady, let's have breakfast on the road; then stop in Franklin and buy a hoagie for our snack," was Jerry's reply.

"A man after my own heart, Doctor Wiley," and she leaned over and kissed him.

They never tired of a ride and talk. At times they seemed to want to make up for the many years they spent before forming this marriage. Fortunately they both felt their lives were perfectly fitted and regretted they had not learned it sooner. They chatted away and seemingly before they knew it they were at Winding Stair Gap, where the AT crosses US64. There were already two cars parked at the trailhead. They had come to recognize cars at trail heads while hiking up from Springer Mountain.

They were only planning to hike about three miles and return the same way. It wasn't the distance, it was the Appalachian Trail. It was already in their blood just like the many hikers they had met. The AT was a community of its own. Men and women have hiked the trail and returned to spend years keeping areas repaired. Some moved close, found work and dedicated their time to assisting hikers. These were considered 'trail angels'.

Most of the hostels on the trail were owned and managed by former thru hikers. It is amazing the comradery Jerry and Sherry were already feeling with the hikers they had encountered. They knew today would be no different.

They did meet one young man, 'CH' or 'Coffee Head'. He had just been discharged from the Marine Corps after a couple tours in Iraq. He said, "I am just hiking to clear my head, and in the mean time getting to know some wonderful folk." He had been awarded the name because he always brewed coffee. No instant java for him.

Sherry was leading the way. After meeting CH they had chatted some but soon both grew silent and into their own thoughts. The trail seemed to do that. It allowed you to clear your head and enjoy the fresh mountain air. Suddenly there was a terrible noise, rustling of leaves and Sherry was startled. Then what looked like a small brown chicken was squawking and flopping its wings as it crossed the trail near her feet. She came to an emergency stop and Jerry about ran into her. The bird went on about twenty feet, stopped and looked back at them.

"What was that all about?" Sherry said, "That scared the wits out of me."

"I think we just witnessed what Pilgrim talked about. We must be close to the Grouse's nest. She is getting our attention away from her eggs or her little ones. Evidently it is not an unusual occurrence on the trail," Jerry answered. They continued their hike.

When they returned to the car they decided to overnight on the road, then take in Fontana in the morning. It was a pleasant evening. They found a mom and pops restaurant and enjoyed some mountain cooking.

The next day found them at Fontana Dam, NC. This was the beginning of the Great Smoky Mountains National Park. They found the trail head parking and read the instructions on the AT post. They learned something they did not know—thru-hikers must list their planned hike and what shelter they plan to spend the night and on which date. Much more detailed than they had thought.

"Oh Jerry, lets walk across the Dam."

"Sure, but from the glint in your eye, you want to climb that Shuckstack Mountain also, right?"

"Well, I had thought about it."

Jerry smiled at his wife, "Let me get a day pack and some water. Then we can walk across the dam."

They did in fact hike up the mountain to what is called The Old Rock Shelter, the oldest in the park. Heading back down the mountain on the very narrow trail, they were surprised to meet two horses with riders. They moved to the side as far as possible. The first rider, an older man, spoke. "Sorry folks my daughter's horse is a little spooked. She just saw a bear back a ways. Please stay calm and bear with us and we will be on out of your way." They were unable to calm the young horse, so the man rode on past and tied his horse. Then he walked back and led his daughter's horse by, but not without some drama. The horse stopped abreast the two hikers and did a little kicking. Fortunately no one was hurt. But being on the lower side in a thicket with no place to move, with the size of the animal, it had been very intimidating.

After the encounter the hikers walked on until they found a good place to stop and take a break. "Now that is strange. The sign below says no animals allowed on the AT through the Smoky Mountains. Then the first thing we run into is not a dog, but a horse. I think we should check on that," said Jerry.

They finished their couple miles down the mountain and started across the dam. As luck would have it they met a Park Ranger. The Ranger welcomed them. When Jerry asked about the 'NO DOMESTICATED ANIMALS' rule. The Ranger smiled, "Well sir, you happened onto the only place in the Smoky Mountains where horses are allowed on the AT. They get to use the first few miles of the trail, then branch off and back down the mountain on another trail. It is an old agreement, older than the AT I think."

They also learned that only hikers with certified requirements can be accompanied by their dogs. Everyone else must kennel their dogs. Shuttles carry the dogs to their owners on the other end in Tennessee.

Back in the car and headed for Mt. Bell Sherry said, "Evidently we will continue to learn, if we continue to hike."

"Yes Sweetheart, and I think I will enjoy the

hike thru the Smoky Mountains. I can't wait to sing 'Rocky Top' when we get up there."

"I'd bet the bears can wait," Sherry said and they both laughed.

Chapter 8

All the planning, reading and dreaming was done. Jerry and Sherry were more prepared now than last year. Now they plan on seven to ten miles a day with some logical breaks. It was simple to find a shuttle with the information they found on the internet and using the Thru-hikers' Companion. They met Tommy, the shuttle driver, at Winding Stair Gap early Monday morning around the first of March.

They enjoyed the conversation and suggestions he gave on the way to Fontana Dam. He suggested getting a motel room at the NOC (Nantahala Outdoor Center), and enjoy watching the canoes as they maneuver the rapids of the Nantahala River.

They were on the trail by ten thirty that

morning. What a great feeling to have the adventure finally start in earnest. This time with much more confidence. This section was about 50 miles with the NOC near the center. They made it to Cable Gap Shelter and were the first hikers there. The seven miles weren't bad. They could have gone further but decided to knock off early and have a camp fire.

Sherry had decided to use 'baby wipes' to bathe. So she made it off into the woods for privacy while Jerry gathered wood for a camp fire. After supper the younger hikers started straggling in. First Jumpstart, Bileau, Sparrow and just a few minutes later came Gunslinger. Pearl and Jen were the last. Everyone was beat. Gunslinger had done the most miles that day topping the list with twenty-two miles.

The Overland Hermits (Jerry and Sherry) enjoyed listening to the young folk. The trail names were still a unique thing for them and they enjoyed learning the why for each one. The camp fire was a luxury, Jerry learned. These kids were worn out, they wanted to eat, chat and curl up for the night. Of course everyone hung their packs, and also hung any food stuffs around the shelter that was not in the pack. By eight in the evening only the old folk were around the fire to put it out. They enjoyed a few minutes of privacy, then they too, crashed. Their first night of many for this year.

Mornings are pretty quiet. Some sleep later than others. Sparrow took off like a flash, snacking on some dried fruit and water. The ssssss of the stoves said some were heating water for oatmeal. Jerry and Sherry had decided on dried fruit and some nuts. After their morning rituals they were anxious to head on down the trail. Since they were walking south, most likely at the speed these kids were traveling, they would be through the Smoky Mountains before the Hermits reached Winding Stair Gap.

It wasn't long until Sherry was ahead of Jerry and they were again in their own world. Each marveling at nature and dreaming of miles and miles of this contentment. They had been on the trail moving south for three hours before they met the first hiker of the day. It was The Wizard. He was asking about Gunslinger and how far ahead he was. He planned to catch him at the first shelter in the Smoky Mountains.

He told them where the next water was and it was good and easy to reach. Of course he asked about his next water source. They were learning to remember those facts because water was life on the trail. The meeting was short. Wizard was off to make some miles.

They took a pack-off break at Hog Back Gap. It was amazing how good the peanut butter crackers and water were. Sherry had also suggested the bite size Milky Way pieces "This is a gourmet meal with dessert," Sherry said.

On down the trail they came to Brown Fork Gap Shelter. They took a break to talk to a couple section hikers there. They all seemed to click. The stories were a lot the same. They were known as Chilly Willy and Just Ray. It was Chilly

Willie who decided they should hike also. Ray would not pick a trail name, but settled for 'Just Ray'. They were retired from the Orlando area. They had thrown logic to the wind and moved into their motor home. Their daughter was house sitting or renting their home. She was their mail service and communications department, Ray said. Now they had parked the motor home to follow Willie's crazy idea. They all laughed as Jerry winked and pointed to Sherry.

They parted and vowed to meet again on the trail and maybe go out for a meal while they took a break. On down the trail 'The Overland Hermits' were in high spirits having met someone of their same age who had decided in the autumn of their lives to hike the AT.

They were able to average ten miles a day until they reached NOC. This was the Nantahala Gorge and they did get a room at the motel. Not a Holiday Inn by any stretch of the imagination, but a place to shower, stretch out on a bed and relax.

Jerry had handled all the cooking which amounted to boiling water for the ramen noodles every evening. The little alcohol stove had worked well but if the wind was up there were times he had to let it cool down, then load more alcohol and finish the job. He hadn't said anything to Sherry yet, but while they were at the NOC Outfitters, he planned to buy one of the little stoves that used the canister gas. Most hikers were using them. He even liked to hear the sound of them. The sound was obvious, a 'sssssss' or 'hissing' sound. It was also much faster than the little alcohol stove. The new stove would be a few ounces, whereas the alcohol stove was less than an ounce. However, weighing the plus side, he would do it.

After a shower and nap they went to the restaurant for a burger. Then over to the Outfitters. Sherry bought another small pack of baby-wipes and Jerry got the stove. Then, they were good to go. They walked back to the restaurant and both got ice cream cones. After enjoying their dessert, they went to watch the canoes and kayakers as they came down thru the white-water. They were both satisfied with the hike this time. The planning had made the difference.

They left NOC early the next morning and were surprised at how light they felt. They made it to Cold Spring Shelter. That was the most they had ever hiked in a day, nearly twelve miles. They both admitted they were tired. Jerry fired up his new stove and was very happy with the results, satisfied he had made the right decision. At the shelter they met 2-Scoops, Turkey Bacon and Snafu. All youngsters between high school and college. Their goal was Mt Katahdin by early September.

Again, everyone enjoyed the campfire and the talk was all about what they had learned so far. Two-Scoops was the only girl. She was doing a solo, but had joined the others a couple miles back. They had met at Standing Indian. The kids got a kick out of the 'Hermits' story of starting the dream at Standing Indian, then dying there. Snafu was a city boy who wanted to learn about the outdoors and eventually be a Ranger in Alaska. Turkey Bacon was a country boy from a small town in Alabama. His dream was to become a doctor and return to his community. The old doctor there was going to help pay for his schooling after promising to come back to the community to practice.

With less than two hundred miles on the AT, The Hermits had met many folks with dreams. Some are jump starting those dreams with a physical challenge. That challenge is to prove to themselves that they can start and complete this project of back packing two thousand miles in one summer and survive a better person.

The next day Jerry feared a blister was forming on his right heel just before they reached Wayah Bald. The AT Data Book indicated a camp site with water and that is where they stopped. They had a very good first aid kit and cleaned the heel, then applied mole-skin. They took their break, ate a pack of cheese crackers and rested. They had come about six miles. Their goal was to overnight at Siler Bald Shelter but they did not make it. They stopped at ten miles and made camp. Strangely, they had passed no north bounders.

Sherry went thru her bath ritual in the tent, while Jerry readied a camp fire and supper. About dusk they saw a young hiker. As she approached she was taking large steady steps. Seeing the tent, she stopped and waved. "Hi, I'm Moonbeam. What do they call you guys?"

"We are the Overland Hermits," Jerry said, "There is plenty of room for your tent here if you are ready to stop."

"Oh no, not ready yet. I'm doing about 5 miles an hour. I will be at the shelter by nine. Gotta make some miles, see ya!" and she was off.

"I am amazed at the single or solo hikers that are female," said Sherry. "This country isn't going to hell in a hand basket as long as we have that kind of youth."

They both enjoyed the peace and quiet. Here they were. The stars were peeping thru the trees, two older love birds chasing a dream and enjoying the time together. It was a strange phenomenon, they were together hiking; at times separated by up to a tenth of a mile, lost in their own thoughts. And then there were times the trail was wide enough for them to walk side by side and share their thoughts. They had the best of both worlds here, solitude and companionship. For humans, that combination is hard to beat.

Off early the next day and Jerry's heel was no problem. They only had about eight miles to Winding Stair Gap and their car. They were light hearted thinking of the next section; about a hundred miles through the Smoky Mountain National Park.

They met 'Weather Carrot' a young man of about twenty five with flaming red hair. The packs came off and they took a break. They brought him up to date on who they had met and gave him the location of a spring about a mile north. Weather Carrot said they had an easy couple miles down to the gap. He was actually a weather man taking a leave of absence and weekly phoning in a report to their small TV station. His audience was pulling for him.

It was amazing how these breaks lifted your spirits even more. The Hermits covered the last couple miles in record time. They were ready to find another motel and some real food. The car was like they had left it. They loaded up and headed to Franklin. Their first section had been a success. Next the Great Smoky Mountains.

Chapter 9

The next day they met a shuttle driver around noon at Davenport Gap in Tennessee. The meeting place was the trail famous Mountain Mama's Café and Hostel. They arranged to leave the car for a couple weeks and the shuttle driver took them back to Fontana Dam. They laughed as they discussed the two hour ride to Fontana Dam with the driver. The funny part was it was going to take the Hermits two weeks to walk back to Mountain Mamas, while taking a short cut thru the National Park.

It was early afternoon when Jerry paid the driver for the shuttle, and they parted. Sherry had thought ahead and had taken one of the required Back Country Permits with them the last time they were here. They had made an estimate of where they would be each night until they reached Tennessee and their car. The Permit was filled out and ready.

They both smiled as they dropped their Back Country Permit in the slot as Jerry said, "Great Smoky Mountains here we come." They headed up Shuckstack, this time with full packs. Many hikers plan to hitchhike into Gatlinburg at Newfound Gap to take a break and restock. Jerry had packed enough food for 14 days. They planned to hike straight through. Most Hikers figure on seven to ten days to walk the National

Park, but at their age, they weren't most hikers.

They pushed themselves and made it to Mollie's Ridge Shelter, but they were two whipped hikers. They did eat, even Sherry skipped the bath ritual. No one else showed up, so they had the shelter to themselves. No camp fire tonight. Sleep was no problem and both of them were still sleeping at around 9 AM when they were awakened by voices. That is how they met Blueberry and Starburst. The Hermits remained in their sleeping bags during the conversation.

B and S were newlyweds, a month now, and they did show affection. Blueberry said, "Some folk have called us BS for short." That brought a rousing laugh. B and S were off towards Rocky Top after topping off their water bottles. Then the Hermits crawled out of their sleeping bags and prepared to face the trail, renewed after twelve hours of sleep!

This time up Shuckstack they met no horses and enjoyed the hike. The one thing different in the Smoky Mountains than the earlier trail is the fact that when you were finally up the mountain, it was called 'ridge running.' Very seldom did they have to go down a mountain and back up, but pretty much stayed up. However they had to descend to resupply the water.

One morning, after spending the night at the shelter where the Cade's Cove trail crosses the AT, Jerry was sitting on a fallen log in front of the shelter. With all morning preps completed, Sherry felt the need to go back to the outhouse. While she was out of sight a young couple walked up coming from Cade's Cove. When they saw Jerry they looked shocked. The girl, glanced at the shelter, then staring at Jerry who was pretty dirty looking and unshaven, asked, "Do you live here?"

Jerry considered saying yes, but opted to tell them he and his wife were hiking the AT. They were shocked to think anyone was planning to walk two thousand miles.

A daily pattern had developed with the

Hermits. After an hour hiking they would take a pack-on break of five to ten minutes. Then after two hours a pack-off break and a snack of bite size Milky Way or Snickers. Another hour or so and a pack off break for a nature call and digging a 'cat hole'. Then a pack of cheese or peanut butter crackers with some cool water. They took one more dried fruit or candy break before stopping around three or four in the afternoon. That usually gave them eight to eleven miles according to the ups and downs.

Ups and downs is where they parted company. Jerry liked the ups and disliked the downs and Sherry was opposite. When they thought they were on Rocky Top, Jerry began to sing John Denver's song. But alas, they were in the clouds and they both learned the meaning of 'false top'. It is a phenomenon all hikers experience when they are tired of going up, the hiker will come to a level area and think this must be the peak, then to find soon after, the terrain starts up again. That day Jerry sang Rocky Top three times. They stopped in the clouds and took a well-deserved break. It was a tough mountain.

They had not seen a bear or deer, but did see a lot of 'droppings'. After about five days they knew they were near Newfound Gap because they came to Clingmans Dome. It is a big point of interest and there were many folk who gave them the once over. Jerry had not shaved in five days. There is a nice tower with good ramps and stairs up. They dropped their packs at the base and made the climb. The trees blocked any view below so visitors climb to get the three hundred sixty degrees view from the tower. Clingmans Dome is the highest point on the trail at 6,643 feet.

Several people asked about the packs and had no idea folks 'walked' thru the Smoky Mountains.

From Clingmans they crossed Love Mountain and spent the night at Mt. Collins Shelter. At times a hiker who is quitting the trail or has too much food will leave it hanging for his fellow hikers. When they arrived, a father and son were already there. After visiting and introducing themselves Jerry asked if the two chocolate puddings hanging up were theirs, or did they want them. Neither claimed nor wanted them. So after supper Jerry and Sherry had dessert.

The next morning The Hermits saw something they would see only once. The fellow campers had fresh eggs, ham and grits for breakfast. They were carrying eighty pound packs. The Hermits left them enjoying their real mountain breakfast.

Next was the famous Newfound Gap, approximately the half way point of the National Park hike. The area was congested. Of course the hikers garnered much attention. They knew Newfound Gap was a big tourist attraction so there must be some vending machines and also some real toilets.

As they expected the Gap was crowded. The parking lot was near capacity. They were looking around for vending machines. They both wanted a Pepsi but no vending machines were in sight. A well-dressed gentleman approached and asked where they were headed. Jerry explained the AT hike and asked the gentleman if he had seen any vending machines. They really wanted a cola of some type.

"Oh, I didn't introduce you to my wife, this is Sylvia. We have a case of Pepsi on ice in the van. Follow me."

"That's all right friend, it isn't necessary."

"Yes it is!" broke in Sherry a little louder than she had meant, "I want a soft drink. Let's follow our new friends." That drew a good laugh from everyone around, and embarrassed Sherry. They continued to talk a few more minutes at the van. They were offered two drinks each but only wanted one. Sherry offered to pay but their benefactors would not hear of it.

They found some shade and broke out the peanut butter crackers and enjoyed the snack, "This tastes so good, mmmmm," said Sherry beaming. "I have grown to appreciate water, but this is a treat."

The Hermits answered a few more questions posed by several youngsters. Then they hefted their packs and continued their hike. About a mile or so they came across a series of rock outcroppings and a magnificent view. "Let's stop here and take a pack off break on one of the outcroppings, sit and enjoy the view. We have plenty of time." This was arguably the best view so far. They were now about two hundred miles from the trail head at Springer Mountain, Georgia.

Enjoying the peaceful setting Sherry said, "Honey, this is so nice. I hope we will do this more often and not rush past the natural beauty we are seeing now."

"I certainly agree Doctor. This is a view to get high on!"

The night's shelter was crowded. They were learning that many folk like to hike the Smoky Mountains. The Hermits pitched their tent and joined everyone as they all were cooking their supper. There were only two other AT hikers, thru-hikers called The Chief and Patchfoot, both from Texas. Of course, there were many questions from the other shelter occupants. The main one was, "How do you find the time?" For the Hermits the answer was simple, retired. The Chief and Patchfoot explained that they had been laid off, their jobs going overseas. They had some money due them from the company profit sharing, and decided to fulfill a goal of theirs while they were still young. The camp fire burned down and everyone went to their sleeping bags.

The next morning Jerry went down to the spring to fill their water bottles. He stood and watched a young boy struggling with a water filter. The boy realized Jerry was watching him, "What are you looking at old man? You never seen a screw-up before?"

"Sure, I have seen lots of screw ups in my life time," said Jerry smiling. "But right now I am looking at a fine young man about to purify some water. I don't see any screw-ups here."

"This hiking and sleeping out in the woods is for the bears not me."

"Then why are you here?"

"The judge says it's gonna make me a better person, yeah right!"

"By the way, my name is Jerry, What do they call you?"

"Johnny, what's it to you?"

Jerry knelt down by the spring and put the hand purifier together for Johnny and said, "The only problem was the in and out were reversed. It will work now."

Johnny started pumping the water thru the filter. "Why do you care anyway? I ain't nothing to you."

They talked for a few minutes, Jerry learned more than he wanted to know, but he could tell that Johnny had potential. It reminded him of his four adopted sons J Leon, Tuck, Buddy and Sticky. On impulse he dug out a business card and a pen. On the back he wrote, 'Contact Dallas Fletcher at Wiley Industries for a full scholarship to a college of your choice.' Johnny had finished filling the water bottles. Jerry said, "Son, you have a lot of potential. In our talk here, which is between you and me, you sounded like you would like to go to college to show the world something. I am going to give you that chance. Not to bitterly show the world something, but to gladly show yourself and the world that you are worth something. If you are serious, give yourself an attitude adjustment right now. Take this card and don't lose it. That little card is worth from twenty thousand to one hundred thousand dollars, according to the college you want to attend."

"What? Is this a joke? It ain't funny."

"No joke son. I am offering to pay your way thru college. I am an old man. I might not be around to see you graduate or even start college, but my word is as good as gold. You contact that number and give them your name. That is all you need to do. But first, YOU must get yourself through high school with grades high enough to get you into college."

"Are you for real?"

"Oh yeah son, I am for real, and you are too."

"Do you think you can get yourself through high school?"

Tears came to Johnny's eyes and Jerry fought them back himself. "Yes sir, I can do that. I didn't know people like you existed," Johnny said as he knuckled his eyes.

"Well, we do. Now wash your face and get back with the group. Smile at the sweet old lady, as you go back, she is my wife ."

Jerry filled the bottles and headed back to camp. He felt light as a feather thinking, *what good is it to have wealth if you cannot share it?*

Jerry was whistling. Sherry was smiling, "Why was the kid, ahead of you on that same path, smiling? He stopped by to say good morning, like he knew a secret."

"He does know a secret. He is a sharp kid. I'll

tell you about it on the trail, but now, we have miles to go before we sleep!" He said smiling.

They were loaded up and ready to leave when a man walked over. "I know you guys are headed out, but can I ask you a question?"

"Sure."

"Johnny is a good kid but he has had a lot of problems in his life. He came back into camp smiling. He even apologized to me. I have never seen him so happy. I am King, his probation officer. Is there something I should know?"

"I'm not sure. It was between Johnny and me. Call him over and we can talk about it."

Johnny came over and said it was okay with him to tell Mr. King, but he would rather everyone not know. The explanation did not take long. Mr. King was thrilled and sort of in shock, like he was trying to fathom what had happened.

Mr. King and Johnny headed back to their group as Jerry and Sherry struck out for the next shelter. "Jerry Wiley, you are one amazing and insightful man. I think Johnny will make something of himself."

"I do also Sweetheart." A pause, "And I am insightful, I married you didn't I?"

The rest of the hike thru the Smoky Mountains was very good. Some great views and they met lots of hikers, BUT they were both smiling when they came to a blue blaze trail to the right with a small sign that read, 'Mountain Mama's' one half mile. They had made it.

At the Café they both ordered the half pound hamburger with mayo, onion, lettuce and tomato with fries. "Now this is the best food I have ever had," said Jerry with a big smile and mayo in the corners of his mouth. Sherry nodded approval as she was chewing the delicious hamburger.

They had decided while they were hiking down on the Blue Blaze trail that they would drive to Erwin, Tennessee. Then get a shuttle back to Davenport Gap and hike north. That would be another hundred miles. They were holding their own and felt good after the hundred miles of the Smoky Mountains.

Chapter 10

The local shuttle driver agreed to pick them up at the Holiday Inn in Erwin, Tennessee at 9AM the next day. He said he knew the Holiday Inn Express would allow them to leave the car there. They also arranged shuttles and assisted hikers. As an added benefit the Inn also gave the hikers a pint of Ben and Jerry's Ice Cream for each night they stayed there. So off they went to Erwin Tennessee.

On the drive to Erwin they discussed storing the car and continuing the hike without the shuttles. There were many points for and against. Of course, if you were strapped for cash, the shuttles could get expensive, but that was not a problem for them. The convenience of having their own transportation, at their age, was reassuring. In the end they decided to continue as they were doing.

The Hermits checked in and arranged storage parking. In the room immediately they dropped the packs on the floor and Sherry started the water into the tub. "I want to soak for hours," she said.

Jerry took his dirty clothes off and lay on the bed covers. He immediately went to sleep and slept until Sherry woke him. "It is your time sleeping beauty or is that Rip Van Winkle?"

"Doesn't matter," he said, "I was being chased through the Smoky Mountains by a giant bear. You saved his life. The bear was about to catch up and that dude would have been in trouble," Jerry was laughing.

Sherry kissed her man and said, "That's the hero I married. Now hit the showers."

Afterwards they found a coin laundry to wash the dirty socks and clothes. They found a restaurant they had heard about on the trail run by thru-hikers of years past. The burritos were giant size, but they had no problem devouring them. Back at the Holiday Inn Express they took the pint of ice cream offered and headed for the room. It would be an early night.

The shuttle was waiting when they walked out a 9AM. They were surprised to see two new hikers talking to the shuttle driver, so they met Sweet Pea and Fire Fly. They were getting a ride down to Allen Gap. On the ride they learned they knew a couple hikers in common, Chilly Willy and Just Ray. Sweet Pea said they were taking a month to do as much as they could of the trail. Both were from Canada. They had been section hiking for five years now and had covered about a thousand miles.

After dropping the other hikers at Allen Gap the shuttle headed for Davenport Gap. Sherry was telling Jerry what Chilly Willy had told her about Sugar Bear and Red Hat. Those hikers were driving a van and using a tow dolly to tow a car. They were leap frogging up the trail. On any given day they would drop the van at a trail head and then drive the car to the next crossing, park the car then hike back to the van to eat and sleep in the van, it was like having their own portable shelter. There was usually some type of road crossing the trail. It can be anything from an interstate to a Forest Service road.

They were at Davenport Gap by ten thirty, then they headed north. Looking at the section map, Jerry commented as they came to a small stream that started from a nice spring, "Sweetheart, as we go down we will be in and out of North Carolina. The west side of the stream is Tennessee and the right side it North Carolina."

In just a few minutes Sherry said, "Honey, watch me jump from Tennessee to North Carolina." As the trail crossed the little two foot wide stream Sherry jumped and they both laughed. The stream grew as they descended and before they reached the bottom it was a good six feet wide of clear mountain water. They knew they were approaching I-40 they had heard the traffic for about a quarter mile now.

Crossing the Pigeon River they heard and saw some folk white water rafting below them. They could also see the over pass with the I-40 traffic. As they approached someone from the interstate blew their horn long and waved like crazy. Right away they knew it was some hikers or want to be hikers. They crossed under the interstate and headed for Deep Gap and the Groundhog Creek Shelter.

What a hike this was. It took them two and a half days to reach Hot Springs, North Carolina. They had climbed five mountains and the most impressive was Max Patch. Of course the views were terrific and all the hikers at the shelters were talking about Trail Days at Damascus, Virginia. Damascus is billed as the friendliest town on the trail. The trail goes right down Main Street. The Hermits started getting Trail Day's Fever themselves.

But this was Hot Springs. They rented a camp site where they were able to shower and wash clothes. They planned to be eating at the local cafés but mainly they scheduled an hour in the hot springs after dinner. This was a treat and interesting also.

The next morning they continued on toward Erwin, crossing the French Broad River before starting up. Jerry had trouble getting boots to suit him. The bottoms of his feet would burn as they hiked. Sherry was having a different problem. She was losing toe nails as they hit the toe of the shoe going downhill. They vowed to get some 'Super Feet' insoles that an outfitter below Blood Mountain had suggested.

The hiking had been good. They were getting more into switchbacks on the steeper mountains. They did not wander into towns like many hikers, because they had their car with more supplies waiting for them. The stories told around the camp fires were always interesting. They had met kids and truckers. One unique family of four was thru hiking while home-schooling.

Passing Lover's Leap they had a great view.

Then up Rich Mountain to the fire tower. The towers always drew Jerry's interest and, if the stairs were not barred, he would climb to the top for a picture and the view. Sherry seldom climbed all the way but she liked the towers.

"Bald Mountain, Little Bald and Whistling Gap," Sherry was taking delight in saying the names of places they passed. She constantly referred to her Appalachian Data Book. It not only gave the names along the trail but the distance from the beginning of the section they were walking to the end of it.

The odd thing to them was that the *Thru Hikers Companion,* which was Jerry's favorite, was laid out starting from Springer Mountain to Katahdin. *The Data Book,* Sherry's preference, was laid out from Katahdin to Springer. Therefore Sherry started at the back of her book. So, by now, Sherry was familiar with reading backwards.

They never tired of seeing the hawks and other

birds soaring beneath them from the higher mountains. The thoughts and beauty of it took their breath away at times. One of the standard comments at times like that was, "We would never see this if we weren't on the trail."

There had been sad times on the hike. They passed the graves of North Carolina boys who had joined the Northern forces in the not-so-Civil War. They had been ambushed and killed at Christmas time as they tried to reach their home in the mountains and share Christmas with their families. They shared their feelings, Sherry from the South and Jerry from the North. "Why couldn't politicians have settled this without a war?" They both knew that Americans had killed more Americans in that war than had been killed in all wars combined.

After the graves they hiked for miles, each lost in thoughts of their dedication to saving lives and the cruelty of wars everywhere.

However, their spirits were lifted when they came upon some members of the Tennessee

Eastman Hiking Club who were doing trail maintenance. What a joy they had hearing the stories of the repair crew. Most of them had been thru-hikers. The work time was casual and they stopped and took a break for a chat. Their love of the Trail and outdoors was infectious. The Hermits learned that the AT is maintained by hiking clubs along the route, all volunteer work.

Just after the encounter they laughed at the name of the next shelter, 'No Business Knob Shelter'. They stopped long enough to refill the water bottles and read the shelter log. They were beginning to recognize names attached to the entries. They pushed on towards Erwin. By now they could judge their progress and barring any unforeseen delays they would be at or past Damascus, Virginia during trail days. They planned to see what the celebration was all about.

At Erwin, they were about one hundred twenty miles from Damascus. They decided to drive to Damascus and spend the night there at a motel, then locate a ride back to Erwin. They found the small town of Damascus to be very interesting—A center for outdoor activities. The AT goes right thru town as it does in many towns. Damascus has gained the title of the friendliest town on the AT. Trail Days is their contribution to hundreds of campers as they converge on the town in the month May.

Damascus is the home of the Virginia Creeper Trail. There are over thirty miles of walking and bike riding trails covering interesting terrain with many bridges and overpasses. So they saw all sorts of bicycles and biking families. Once in Damascus they opted for the Methodist Church Hostel instead of a motel. The hostel is touted on the trail as a great place for hikers.

Chapter 11

They had a day or two to spend in Damascus so they decided to walk around and get a lay of the land. The first item was to purchase 'Superfeet' insoles. The Salesman who had been a thru hiker said many folk used the Superfeet in walking or running shoes. He again quoted the often heard adage, 'On the AT, you hike your own hike using what is most comfortable to you.' People have hiked in all manner of shoes, even a few have done it barefoot.

After leaving the outfitters Jerry spotted something interesting at the local service station; an older van with a raised top with a tow dolly attached. The two were advertised 'For Sale'. It was a slow day at the station and they took their time in making a deal. When they were finished Jerry had bought an older used car that the manager declared would tow with all four wheels on the ground. Then Jerry traded the tow dolly for the work and tow kit for the old car. That way parking would be less of a problem and the car would tow behind the van nicely. The manager said it would be no problem to store their car until someone could pick it up and he could have the car set up and ready before his busy time at trail days. Jerry and Sherry were happy campers. Locating a shuttle was no problem and before long they were back in Erwin and on the AT again.

The river that runs thru Erwin is the Nolichucky. They both loved the name. The Shuttle dropped them at the river crossing. However, The first shelter was too soon to overnight so they hiked to Beauty Spot Gap. There was a great place to tent camp with water nearby. They were both feeling their bodies hardening and gaining more muscle. The views were fantastic. Roan Mountain in Tennessee was a tough climb and at times it seemed straight up, but with small trees to grab and assist they made it. The views at the top were awesome.

Walnut and White Rock Mountains gave them time to pause and enjoy the beauty. A little over a week of the Northward hike they came to US321. They both smiled and hugged. Cars drove by honking at the old hikers as they smiled and waved. The drivers did not know that they were looking at the Watauga Lake. The place where it first began. Crossing the road they made it to the very table they had been having the picnic when they met Half pint. Sherry said, "Sir, do you mind if I drop my pack here? I see a real rest room!" They both burst out laughing. People were looking at them as they waved and headed for the real toilets.

After taking the toilet break they sat and had some crackers and water. Smiling and remembering that first day. They were like kids. Before they headed out they had a chance to tell some locals the inside joke they had been laughing about. This time they went across the dam and up into the mountains. In four days they were back in Damascus a day before Trail Days was to begin. They had walked by Shady Valley, Tennessee, McQueen's Knob and Abington Gap before reaching the Tennessee/Virginia border. That was four miles before Damascus.

They took possession of their new home and car. At the advice of the station owner they went to Herb's Campground and parked on the creek bank. The van was a great place to sleep. Had a small closet and even a porta pot. The rear doors opened to a big icebox and more storage. "This is going to be great," Sherry exclaimed. Jerry agreed. They were a couple miles out of town but with their new tow vehicle, it was no problem.

Trail Days is a giant festival. Hikers from all over the world show up. Many thru-hikers from years past are drawn like a bug to a light, to the atmosphere of hiking. Venders were hawking everything about hiking and camping. There were lectures, classes, gifts, contests and every type of food known to man. There is also a Boot Camp where your foot is analyzed and custom 'Superfeet' insoles created just for you.

There were giveaways, entertainment and music all day. They ran into several hikers that had passed them on the trail. They even had an evening with Chilly Willy and just Ray.

They did not stay the full time. Both Sherry and Jerry were ready to try out this leap frog hiking. Checking the maps, they settled on driving the car to Creek Junction Station, VA highway 728. With a map on her lap Sherry directed Jerry to the very rough trail head. They had to hunt for a parking site. This was going to be their test. On the first try with day packs only they were shooting for 13 miles. They looked the last time at their tow car and headed south. From now on they would actually be going north walking south. It was a good walk and the trip without the heavy backpacks was much easier, but it was still no walk in the park. They took regular breaks and enjoyed the scenery. They crossed Straight Mountain and walked across Highway 58. Many Hikers go into Abington on number 58. They passed Woodman and Moses who had also left Trail Days early to get ahead of the crowd. Paha was down the trail closer to Damascus. He declared his love for the woods and to walk by himself and enjoy his religion, which was nature.

It was late in the day when they reached the

camper but still decided to find the next road crossing North of where their car was located and spend the night. They headed north and Sherry was directing her designated driver to VA600 at Elk Garden, giving them a ten mile hike back to the car. They found a good parking spot at the trail head, fixed supper and both turned in early. "I think you came on a great idea Mrs. Wiley. My compliments for your brilliant idea. Now we have a portable motel." They were both asleep minutes after it got quiet.

In the next few days they were able to park and hike 8-12 miles with the day packs. It was very interesting hiking through Grayson Highland State Park. Here they saw wild horses and cattle. They learned this was one of the few places in the eastern USA where this was a reality.

As in every dream a little rain must fall. After having such a good time they decided to take a big chunk of trail and do some back packing. The spot they picked would wind by what was called *God's Thumb Print* in Virginia. They had heard of the beauty of the trail and streams along the way. They parked the car and headed south. They weren't happy about fording creeks. It had happened before. Sherry had purchased a new pair of boots at the boot-camp in Damascus. The creek was forded at least four times that day as it crisscrossed the trail. That night, at a shelter, Jerry made the mistake of drying Sherry's boots over the camp fire.

The next day after reaching the mountain heights and walking the trail as it over looked the valley, Sherry was having trouble with her heels. They stopped above a water source and Jerry descended the 50 yards for water. When he returned, Sherry had tears in her eyes and she was bare foot. Her heels looked terrible. Not blisters, just red and hurt deep. It was around noon.

They decided to set up camp early and rest for the day. It turned into a few days and her heels got no better. It was a beautiful camp site. They had time to read and talk to thru hikers. They met Tin Man and Godiva, NOBOs (North Bounders) who offered some vitamin I. Jerry took one just in case they ran out of their own supply.

God's Thumbprint is actually Burke's Garden. It's a place of extraordinary beauty in Tazewell County, Virginia. Burke's Garden was a possible site for the Vanderbilt's southern home, but Asheville, North Carolina won out and is now the home of the Biltmore Estates, instead of Burke's Garden.

Sherry's heels got a little better and they took a chance to leave the camp site. After several frustrated attempts, due to cell signals, they made contact with a shuttle to get a ride back to the Van. They took a few days in a motel to relax, buy some walking shoes then headed on north. The amazing beauty of each state takes your breath away. They hiked thru the Shenandoah National Park. On one occasion in the Shenandoah's Sherry said, "Look to your left Jerry." Looking over he spotted a large doe lying about ten feet off the trail just watching them go by. They laughed because usually it is humans watching the animals.

Once in Virginia three large goats came between Sherry and Jerry. They hiked along until all of a sudden the goats jumped into the bushes and were gone. They hiked the 'Roller-coaster' just before Harper's Ferry, West Virginia. The Roller-Coaster is small mountains or big hills with many ups and downs in a row. Harper's Ferry is the home of the 'Appalachian Trail Conservancy'. At the time they hiked through, the 'C' was for Conference. There are only a few miles of the trail in West Virginia and there they crossed the Shenandoah River on a highway bridge. They had hiked a little over a thousand miles.

Through the few miles in Maryland and into the huge state of Pennsylvania, where they overnighted at Pine Grove Furnace State Park. This is the half way point of the AT. Here they learned the tradition of eating a half gallon of ice cream. A point mentioned by The Pilgrim a thousand miles back when he said, "Eat a half gallon of ice cream for me." They did share a half gallon, after all it was a tradition. They sat in the little State Park Store with several hikers as they all ate ice cream and rehashed their journey to the half way point.

The beauty of Pennsylvania, Jerry's home state, came closer to them in spite of learning close up of the rocks of Rocksylvania, the state where boots come to die. Hiking beautiful mountains, walking thru apple groves and across Amish farm lands, they crossed the beautiful and mighty Susquehanna River at Duncannon. They had walked thru battlefield and old coal field towns. Oh yes, and had sampled some delicious Pennsylvania Dutch cooking. This was actually the most Jerry had seen of his state up close and personal. He was proud. As they were leaving the state they met another Freight Train. The first person they had met hiking for a cause. He was representing Kyle Petty Racing. Mainly he was bringing attention to the Victory Junction Gang Camp for terminally ill children. Kyle had given him time off during the racing season and even met him at one junction and took several hikers to a motel for baths and dinner. They enjoyed an evening with Freight Train around the camp fire with Skywalker, Dude, Paint Brush and Blue Heron. Freight Train's enthusiasm was catching. Jerry was determined to remember the Charity.

Leaving the van in New Jersey, they drove into New York on Long House Road. Next up on the AT map is New York and a real surprise to Sherry, there is more to New York than New York City.

Chapter 12

"This is New York? Where are the sky scrapers and all that city stuff?"

"You are in New York State my love, not New York City. There is actually a lot of country in this state. But your impression is normal, most folks down south think of the north as only cities." Jerry answered as they turned onto New York 17A. Today would be a hike of less than ten miles, but over the highest point of the AT in New York, Prospect Rock.

Before the trailhead Jerry pulled into a quick stop for gas. The stop also had a deli. Sherry went inside to look around and came out smiling. In one hand was a paper sack and in the other was a pastry. "Sweetheart, these smelled good and they taste heavenly. The lady inside bakes them. You are gonna love it." And of course he did. That was Sherry's introduction to the New York outside the City. She continued to sing the lady's praises of being a good cook and southern friendly. There was plenty of parking at the trail head, so they suited up and headed south back into New Jersey. Prospect Rock was the last climb and descent before reentering New Jersey. It was such a pleasant walk, they weren't winded. Hiking with the lighter day packs made life easier for the old hikers.

They slept in the van at the trail head. Tonight there was a light tap on the window. It was a local law enforcement officer just checking to see if they were ok. Jerry and the officer passed a few minutes and the officer took his leave with a, "You guys have a good hike through our great state."

On the fourth day in New York they had found a very narrow road at the trail head. They squeezed the van into a tight spot and again started south. They were pleasantly surprised as they left the road and walked into The Graymoor Spiritual Life Center, home of the Franciscan Friars. It was early as they followed the AT blazes across the campus. On the second path they met a Friar. He was a pleasant man and introduced himself as Father Callahan. They chatted and when he found out Sherry was from Belmont he smiled, "Ah, home of the Belmont Abbey. You being Protestant would not have known one of my best friends, Father O'Shields.

He lived and passed there, rest his soul." Looking at Jerry, "You are smiling my friend, have I said something amusing?"

"Father, you have no idea. Yes, heavens YES, Father O'Shields was the breath of Christ, I knew him well." For an hour they sat and talked as Jerry related his relationship with Father O'Shields.

"The Overland Hermits are welcome to spend the day and night with us. We also treat the thru hikers to dinner if you would stay."

"You are such a breath of fresh air yourself Father Callahan, and thank you very much for the invite but I will escort my bride on down the road, but please could I have a card. We would love to send a gift to the Graymoor Friars." After receiving the card they said goodbye. The hike on down to the Bear Mountain Bridge was just a delightful time as they discussed the amazing AT and how Jerry had met a friend of a friend just in passing on a trail.

They enjoyed the view of the Hudson River as

they crossed. Years ago the toll for a pedestrian was five cents, now only vehicles pay a toll. Just across the bridge they were also very surprised to see The Trailside Museum and Zoo. That was the second pleasant happening and it was still early in the day.

They had plenty of time so enjoyed the animals and especially the huge statue of Walt Whitman. They both smiled at the name. They had met a middle aged hiker who called himself 'Uncle Walt', as in Walt Whitman. He was an enjoyable character. He was hiking about their speed and they had passed him several times. He was ahead of them now they thought. Meeting him here would have been really against the odds.

They climbed Bear Mountain. It is the second highest point on the AT in New York at 1,305 feet. They stopped by the West Mountain Shelter to read the log and take a break. Hemlock and Tia were stopping for the night. The Hermits had met them back in Damascus. Tia and Hemlock were having a 'discussion'. All Jerry heard Hemlock say was, "That is impossible!"

"Whoa kids, what is the problem?" said Jerry laughing.

"Tia says she saw a giraffe on the trail. Do you believe that?"

"Wait, did you say a giraffe? And was it just after the Shenandoah's?" asked Sherry.

"Yes, and I know I saw it but just for a second."

"We did too!" said Sherry.

"Come on," pleaded Hemlock, "Not you too!" Sherry explained about the National Zoo having an area for the zoo animals to recuperate from injuries or medical reasons. The AT goes right by the area. "We were assuming the giraffe was the only animal that could be seen over the fence."

"Okay, being ganged up on like this, I apologize Tia!"

"Well I am just glad the Hermits stopped by so I don't think I am crazy. I was beginning to wonder." Everyone had a good laugh. After a short visit and check of the log the Hermits continued south to their car. It had been a great day. On the way back to the van in New York, they stopped by Peekskill and treated themselves to a NY pizza. It was delicious!

New York continued to be a good hike. Meeting hikers was one great thing about hiking south but going north. They continued to take the car or van eight to twelve miles to a trail head and hike back south. Then drive north again passing the van or car for a day's hike and coming back south to the other vehicle. About weekly they found a motel for a good bath and sit down meal. For older folk this was an ideal way to hike the AT. They never fooled themselves thinking that they were doing the same as the thru-hikers, but they were seeing the same sights.

For the last few miles of New York they drove just inside the Connecticut State Line and parked on Connecticut route 55.

On this AT hike they had crossed roads, rail

roads, interstates, rivers and creeks. A few miles out of Connecticut they put a new wrinkle in their horn. They came to the Metro North Railway. At the crossing in the middle of a field was a small lean-to at the trail crossing. The sign read: "Appalachian Trail Railroad Station". From here the AT hikers could take the train into New York City, and many did. Smiling, Jerry said, "Now that is service!"

The AT continues. Next state is Connecticut. At the state line they have hiked 1,440 miles. Not bad for old folk in their seventies.

Chapter 13

The State of New York had definitely not been a disappointment. They drove past their car and on to Kent, Connecticut where they would overnight at the trail head. Once settled they used their head lamps to read a little before turning in. Sherry was looking at the AT section map for Conn/Mass, "It looks like we are going to start into some steeper mountains right away, according to the tail profiles," she said. " It is amazing how the terrain can change."

"Yeah I remember what SOBO's (South Bounders) Lynn and He-man said in the Shenandoah's. 'Just wait until you see the Whites, especially the Presidential Range'. I am sorta looking forward to it."

"I'm not sure that I am ready, but I am anxious to see them. They keep talking about hiking above the tree line. That will definitely be different." It wasn't long until both lights were out and they cuddled in the little three quarter bed. It was close quarters but much more comfortable than the pads on the ground.

There was a small deli close to the trail head so they drove over before heading off on the day's hike. Jerry had a ham and egg croissant and Sherry had the yeast roll with bacon, egg and cheese. Both were lip smacking good. Business was slow and they enjoyed chatting with the cook. She had some tales of hikers that stopped by over the years. She had met Bill Irwin and his dog Orient. Bill is the only blind hiker that had hiked the trail. The Hermits had read his book 'Blind Courage', a best seller about his famous AT hike. Betty had a picture of her, Bill and Orient posted on the wall along with the many hikers that stopped by. She snapped a quick picture of the Overland Hermits. They took a coffee to go, said good bye to Betty and made it back to the trail head before nine.

Mount Algo was their first climb out of Kent. It topped out close to fifteen hundred feet. It was not very high compared to mountains they had climbed, but since Pennsylvania, not many climbs had been steep. The land above the Housatonic River was nice and once up they did get to do some ridge running. Connecticut has about fifty miles of AT. Every one they met was saying, 'this is getting us ready for the Whites'.

The AMC Connecticut Chapter Hiking club maintains the trail in the state and does a great job. They did get to meet one crew working on some steps. Moving the huge rocks into place took a lot of leverage and muscle. Every hiker seemed to take time to thank them for the work. And like the workers further south, most of these volunteers were prior thru hikers.

The last hike in Connecticut took them nearly 2500 feet over Bear Mountain. When they arrived at the Limestone Spring Lean-to for a break, three hikers were already there taking a break—Bearboy, Mr. President and Mooseburger. It was easy to see how Mr. President got his name. He looked very much like Bill Clinton. He was very good natured and pretty good with some impersonation quips. Bearboy was another story. He said at one shelter in the Smoky's he left his pack on the ground to use the out-house. He returned to find a bear with his pack. He said he was crazy enough to try to wrestle the pack away but the bear won. He was not hurt but said the bear tore the pack and ate all the food while he stood and watched, then walked off.

He said other hikers shared their food until he reached Newfound Gap where his parents replaced his stuff and begged him to quit, but he went on. That was quite the story. But the real kicker was Mooseburger. He was a big man, late fifties and in great shape. He had a heavy German accent. Once he started talking there was no stopping him. Old Mooseburger had been and done everything, and at every job (it came out as 'chob') he was the best there was, there was no better. Once the president himself had sent Air Force One to pick him up to compete against the Russians in a shooting contest, because he was the best there was. Jerry said later to Sherry, "In all honesty, out here you could be talking to a governor or CEO of a large company. I have learned in life to accept a man at his word until I have reason to doubt him. Mooseburger may be a BS artist or a man who can do what he says, with a big ego."

Hikers on the trail are congenial and seldom condescending. Just folks out to hike and enjoy nature. Jerry and Sherry met hikers from many countries and walks of life. From heavy equipment operators to doctors. They encountered ladies, many of them nurses, walking alone from sixteen to eighty-two years of age. In the Smoky's they met the pastor of a large church in Knoxville. He said being out in the mountains alone gave him freedom and a clear head.

The hike in Connecticut was a little tough, but with over 1400 miles under their belt, they were anxious to continue on. Life just didn't get much better than this. This old couple never tired of a little smooching in the middle of the trail. They were enjoying their life.

****

Massachusetts—the home of the Kennedys. Of course the AT covers about seventy miles in Mass, but on the opposite side of the state from Cape Cod Bay. The mountains become a little tougher and take a little more out of older hikers. But the going was still good. They seldom found a spot where they needed to backpack, and that was only at the most two nights out. The joy of overnighting was meeting and the fellowship with other hikers. Many times The Hermits would give their fellow hikers rides into town for resupply.

Sherry had called for their mail on the average of every two weeks and had it delivered general delivery at a small town on the way. Jerry had rigged up his laptop with the cell phone and since Pennsylvania they had been able to get and send e-mails most of the time.

One morning near North Adams, Massachusetts Jerry woke up with a fever and chills. A couple days earlier he had found a tick had attached itself to his privates. They had removed the tick and sterilized the area. But the symptoms he was showing, they knew, were that of Lyme Disease. So immediately Sherry drove them into North Adams to the hospital and he checked into the emergency room. Unlike any emergency room they had ever been in, Jerry was the only patient awaiting help. Within a few minutes he was seen by a doctor who took blood samples and told them, of course, it could be Lyme. He would not be sure until the blood work came back. He prescribed the treatment for Lyme anyway, saying that if it wasn't Lyme it would not bother him, but if they waited and it was Lyme, it would be too late for the meds to work effectively. They left with instructions and a prescription.

They first found a campground and stayed there a day. Then they decided this was going to take longer so they did get a motel for three days. Sherry only left her Jerry to go get meds and food.

Four days later the doctor called, "No sign of Lyme, drop the Lyme meds and use only the pain and fever meds. If it continues past seven days, report back. On the fifth day Jerry was ready to attack the AT again, both relieved that it had not been Lyme Disease.

During the illness the crew from Jerry's old

Corporation the MVA (Modern Vigilante Association) kept in contact, ready to help evacuate or do anything necessary. Jerry smiled as he told Sherry, "Those sneaky guys have been keeping an eye on us, and I would bet Dallas, back at Wiley Industries, is responsible."

Unknown to Jerry and Sherry some of the hikers they had met were company agents assigned to keep an eye on the 'Overland Hermits'. Dallas told Tuck, Buddy, Sticky and J Leon (Jerry's adopted sons) that what happened in the Mediterranean will not happen again. Jerry and his wife are too valuable. Dallas was referring to a vacation Jerry and Sherry had taken on which Jerry was kidnapped and came close to dying if the MVA had not moved in to solve the problem. Several Terrorists had been eliminated while Jerry and a yacht crew were rescued. Dallas was retired but still held the reins of Jerry's 'Wiley Industries' out of Pittsburg.

Massachusetts had also given them another reminder of the dangers associated with the AT.

They had parked at the trailhead on Jug End Road and spent the night in the van. The car was parked just behind them. The next morning they drove the car twelve miles ahead at the next road crossing and hiked back. When they arrived back at the van another hiker had parked behind them, just where their car had been the night before. It was more than likely a section hiker. They stood with their mouth's open. A giant pine tree had fallen and crushed the Jeep wagon that had parked behind the van. If they had driven the van and not the car, the car would have been demolished.

In a few minutes a local law enforcement officer arrived. They helped clean up the broken glass. A crew arrived and cut the tree off the Jeep. The officer left a note for the owner to explain what had happened. Jerry and Sherry never did see the unfortunate hikers.

Mount Greylock was their toughest mountain in Massachusetts It peaked at around 3500 feet. The news carried by the SOBOs was, 'you ain't seen nothing yet. The Whites are FUN.'

Chapter 14

Vermont is beautiful. It has hilly farm land along with beautiful mountains. They hiked thru pastures and by neat small grave yards. Most of the small creeks and streams had nice walking bridges. Crossing most of the pasture fences was accomplished by steps built up and over the fence versus the angled openings used further south. The angle openings were tight to get through, but not enough for cows and horses to maneuver.

There was actually one sign on an obvious 'short cut' on the trail. To suppress hiker's desire to cut across the unauthorized field the farm had posted a sign that read: "If you think you can cross in 30 seconds, remember the bull can do it in 10." That one drew a smile.

Some of the hills and mountains gave amazing picture post card images of white homes and steeple'd churches in calm, green valleys. They were also treated to an education on how the Vermonters drew the maple 'sap' for the famous Vermont Maple Syrup. The trees were tapped and attached to a plastic hose. The hose went from tree to tree as it descended the mountain. The hose increased in diameter as it went down and fed into huge 100 gallon tanks. No longer did the Vermonters go from tree to tree to empty buckets hanging there as seen in the history books. The Hermits were equally amazed at the process.

Entering Vermont the AT joins the Vermont Long Trail for about a hundred miles. The Long Trail covers Vermont from south through the Green Mountains to Canada and is the oldest long distance trail in the United States. The Long Trail (LT) is about six years older than the AT.

The Hermits had not seen a bear since the beginning of the trail almost sixteen hundred miles ago. They did not see a bear in Vermont but smelled a couple. They are easy to recognize after a rain. You can tell a bear just crossed the trail from the strong smell they leave. After looking at the trail maps they did not think that they would be overnighting on the trail in Vermont, but the 'Thru Hiker's Companion' noted that some camp sites charged $6 a night to cover maintenance expense.

While near Bennington Jerry got to visit the headquarters of 'Hemming Motor News'. It was a treat for him because he subscribed to the paper which was about antique cars. They also staffed a 'full-service' service station. Pulling in you got the service from the 1950's. With a fill-up your windshields were washed and the oil was checked. The whole set up took them back in time. It was a neat break from the hike.

The one thing they had been surprised at was the number of swamp or marshlands from New York north. Both Jerry and Sherry had associated that landscape with the south. Some of the trail was so swampy that hundreds of yards of board walk was constructed to protect the environment.

Jerry had this great idea that turned sour. When they came to Mount Killington there was a ski lift to the top. It stood at 4,000 feet. Why not drive to the lift, take it to the top and hike south. Then drive past it and hike up the North Slope to the lift and take it down. They both agreed it was a good idea.

They took the lift up. It was a fun ride, neither were skiers, so this was different. The lift operators pointed them in the direction of the AT and they started down. The trail went down a ski slope for many yards. They were both amazed at the size of the rocks that would be covered with snow in the winter and skiers would go over them.

The problem arose in the woods on the trail down. The area was scattered with huge rocks. Suddenly, Sherry gasped as she stepped down off a large rock. She had pulled a groin muscle. Fortunately they did carry the first aid pack. Jerry immediately gave her an 800 mg 'vitamin I'

(Ibuprophen). They found a spot to relax for an hour or so until Sherry could walk without much pain, and continued on down.

Back to a motel for a few days so Sherry could recuperate. It was Jerry's time to play doctor and care giver. He was also the rehab therapist and did a lot of muscle massaging. They had no problem reading, relaxing and enjoying the local cuisine. After all, this was all part of the adventure.

They had time to talk, something they always enjoyed. They laughed at the places they had encountered the snoring and non-snoring shelters on the trail. Laughed at a rainy time early on the trail, that Jerry had gotten up in the night to relieve himself and returned to his sleeping bag in the shelter to find 'Mieska', a very wet blonde Labrador, in his sleeping bag. Mieska belonged to a fellow hiker who was asleep. A good story, but a wet night for Jerry. They were laughing when Jerry's cell phone rang.

*********Phone Call********

"Hi Jerry, this is Dallas, how is the hike going?"

"Great Dallas, good to hear from you. Well, right now, it isn't going too well for Sherry. She has a pulled groin muscle."

"OUCH, but where are you now?"

"We are in a motel near Killington Mountain, actually we are in Rutland, Vermont. Our plans are to be here a few days until Sherry is feeling better."

"I hate it for our First Lady, but good for me. I need your signature on some papers and my Power of Attorney will not work in this instance. You need to see these papers anyway."

"Let me check the best way to do this, and get back to you. Got an address handy?" said Dallas.

"Yeah, hold on one, I have the motel card here," pause, " Here we are." Jerry filled him in on the address.

"This may take a couple days, I will check FedEx and UPS. Let me get back to you. Take care of the First Lady."

"Count on it. Love to Marian." The call ended and Jerry filled Sherry in on the details.

The motel stay was agreeing with Sherry. With rest, heat and regular meals she was mending well. Jerry used the time to work on their hiking gear and wash clothes.

The next day Dallas called again. "Hey dude, I need a break. It has been a long time since Marion and I have been to Vermont, so we decided to come see you. I have reservations at the Hampton Inn. We will be there at 1600 hrs. If you guys can come down, it will save us renting a car."

"No problem there Dal, Sherry will be thrilled to spend some time with Marion. That may be just what she needs."

The phone call ended and after hearing about Marion, Sherry was on a high. "This will be great, I am glad Dallas decided to come up."

The next day, dressed in their best hiking clothes, they drove down to the hotel. The concierge said Dallas was awaiting them and escorted them to a room and opened the door. Puzzled, the Hermits looked at each other, they followed the concierge inside, and it was dark. Then suddenly the lights came on to group singing, "For they are jolly good fellows....etc.."

There was a huge banner that read:

Congratulations

Hiking 1680 miles on the AT

Surprised is not the word for how they felt. Flabbergasted would have been better. As they looked around they saw family and friends. It looked as if everyone they knew was here.

After a lot of hugging and friendly joking, Dallas called for order and he took the podium. "Sherry, we all are so proud of you to have harnessed my boss. He tells me he is the happiest he has ever been and I know that is saying a lot. When I approached your adopted sons with this idea, they jumped at the chance to see you. The word spread and the number wanting to come exceeded the Gulfstream so we needed a larger aircraft. Don't have a heart attack, Jerry. We didn't have time to buy a 707, but we did borrow one from your friend Mr. Belk. He said "Hello" by the way and "best of luck." So let's enjoy the dinner and have a lot of fellowship."

Sherry was thrilled. Evelyn, Dianne, Dean, Rose and Jo Ann her class mates were there. Shirl a friend and DI, Rose and Josephine the wives of the boys were there. J Leon's wife could not make it.

It seemed all of the MVA members had made it. Tuck, Buddy, J Leon and Sticky. Then many of the main cogs in the machine were there, Mark, Matt, Luke, Sherece, Stephen, Jennifer, Joshua, Megan, Ben, Elsie and Stella. Sherry's brothers Johnny and Vernon were there also.

Chilly told Sherry that Mr. Fletcher had gotten in touch with them through Sugar Bears Trail Journal and had invited them.

What a day. Sherry forgot the muscle pull. She was on a high. She was one to appreciate friends and Jerry was one to appreciate the men and women who had made his life a joy, and successful.

The last surprise. Showing up with packs and hiking gear was Blaze, Little Forest, Moonshine and Pickle. "We saw a sign on the trail that there was free food here, The Overland Hermits treat!" Blaze called out as they came in. Everyone applauded. The Hermits had met these hikers several times on their hike.

As they headed back to the motel Sherry and Jerry were on a plain above happy. It was a feeling of, 'I am loved'. There was no explaining that feeling.

Soon they were back on the trail and had crossed the Connecticut River into New Hampshire. They would start their hike just west of Hanover and hike back through Dartmouth College. They did not take advantage of the offers, but hikers can overnight and eat at the college. They were now in the great state of New Hampshire, home of the famous White

Mountains. This meant they had hiked, albeit mostly leap frogging, over 1700 miles.

Looking at the 1700 mile figure, Sherry asked Jerry, "Can you believe that two old folk have hiked 1700 miles?"

Taking her in his arms out in the woods he said, "Yes, sweetheart I can believe it. You are some lady, Doctor Wiley. I am so glad I found you in time to have this much fun in the autumn of my life." The Overland Hermits enjoyed this moment with a long kiss. Life for them was good.

Having married late in life, Jerry and Sherry were very compatible. They both wanted to savor the years they had left. They were under no illusion that they would live forever on this earth.

Chapter 15

With their car across the Connecticut River in Norwich, Vermont, the Hermits parked at the trail head on Three Mile Road. The hike back to the car would have a lot of town and road walking because they would be walking through Dartmouth College and Hanover, New Hampshire. Jerry fixed the evening's ramen noodles then they relaxed and read some. Sleep came easy to the senior couple. To finally have real love in their lives, sleep was good and the cuddling was like an answer to prayer.

Just before going to sleep, Sherry raised on one elbow and looked down at her husband, "You know Jerry, with all the wealth at our finger tips, your family mansion in Pittsburg and a modest home in Mount Bell, I am just as happy here as any place on earth. This old van and a three-quarter bed, while cuddling with the sweetest man in the world beside a country road in New Hampshire, is better than a queen's castle."

"Doctor Wiley, Mrs. Wiley, I share your sentiments. But the wealth, the mansion and all we have is OURS. Lady, we are a team." Pulling her off her elbow into his arms he whispered,

"You have made this old man the happiest guy in the world. YES, a million times YES, this van is our castle." Holding his love close he added, "Without you I was wealthy but empty. You have filled a void that has been crying for you for years. I love you." They fell asleep lost in a world of their own thoughts.

They both smiled as they passed through Dartmouth. Seeing the young lives filled with dreams and plans for the future, they knew they were looking at the normal college cross section of youth with dreams of a great future—Young folk that were determined to make the world a better place and, of course, the bright eyed energetic kids in college for all the fun that comes with being in college.

Like all AT hikers they were always looking for the white blaze that indicated they were still on the AT. The convention of two blazes together indicating a change in directions or a turn in the trail was an automatic signal to 'pay attention.' The blaze was on power poles, trees, bridge abutments and at times on the pavement.

Only a couple times in over 1700 miles had they missed the blaze and had to back track to get back on the trail. They had been surprised at how fast the one hundred fifty miles in the state of Vermont had passed, even with the pulled groin muscle. Vermont, so far, was their pick of fairly tough mountains and extremely beautiful pastoral scenery. The Green Mountains were tough but not an impossible challenge.

They picked up the car and stopped to pick up a pizza as they had often done to enjoy back at the van. It was one of the perks of Sherry's idea of 'leap-frogging'. Many of the thru-hikers smiled at the 'old folks' type thru-hike. Most commented on it being a good idea, if you could afford it. The Hermits knew, however, that there was the 'purist hikers' that thought any comfort ideas on a thru-hike were taboo. No matter the feelings of individuals, the spirit of the AT is to get out, enjoy nature and face the challenge of the 2170 miles of natural beauty.

The hike continued over Moose Mountain. Then they had to strap on the back packs for a couple days to get over Smarts Mountain and Mount Cube. They reached over three thousand feet with some tough climbs. The night after backpacking those two, Sherry was looking at the upcoming mountain profiles. It was the famous Moosilauke, the first of the biggies. It reached forty eight hundred feet. "Honey, would you mind if I set out Moosilauke, I don't think I am ready."

"Certainly not honey, we will both take a break if you like. Maybe we need the rest before attacking the Whites."

"No, I think I could drop you off on the north end and drive back to Glencliff and wait for you. I know you are ready to climb, and I can relax and read and not feel like I am an anchor."

Jerry climbed Moosilauke. The north slope runs right beside a good sized branch, and basically straight up. It is at time perilous because the wooden blocks that are attached to the rock face with rebar, are very slick because of the dampness from the branch. The hike without his 'girl' wasn't as much fun. He missed her. As he walked, he was thinking about this team, Sherry and Jerry. *No sweetheart, if this is the end of the hike so be it, but the idea of this hike is us. If the Whites are the end, so be it. This has been a fun ride.*

Moosilauke was in the clouds. This was the first mountain above the tree line and Sherry was not here to enjoy it. It was very hard to see in the mist. The only thing that kept him on the trail was the rock cairns that had been stacked with the AT blaze prominent.

The down was not bad. Jerry had long since cut the ends of his walking shoes so his toe nails did not hit the ends of his shoes. His feet were slim and it was hard for him to tie the shoe so his foot would not slide, even with the 'Super Feet' insoles.

It even surprised him at how good he felt to see their van and Sherry getting out to give him the congratulatory hug. As they hugged he said,

"I missed you. I don't plan on doing any more solos."

They did take a couple days off and took I-93 north to see where the Old Man of the Mountain had been. They were disappointed that the Old Man had been there for thousands of years, but before their arrival had lost his hold and fell. The fateful date was May 4th 2003. He had been a fixture and an Identification landmark to the state since before joining the Union as the ninth state in 1788.

They did other sightseeing. Grafton Notch and Franconia Notch State park have some interesting sights for AT hikers and the many tourists. The Flume Gorge with its spectacular water falls where loggers sent logs down the river. The basin that thousands of years of wear in rock have made the perfect bowl. The Bridal Falls are amazing and many more sights. The Hermits were relaxed and had had a plan. They were ready for the toughest AT challenge, the White Mountains.

Chapter 16

To attack the Whites, the first hike would require some backpacking. They left the van at Franconia Notch on US 3. Their destination was Crawford Notch on US 302. It was easy to locate the AT and the famous white blaze. What a great day. The hike was good, an easy up and it leveled off at about 2500 feet. They were in great spirits and the trail was wide enough for side by side hiking for much of the way. They had a late start so after about six and a half miles they tried to locate a good camp site that fit the rules, but could not. There was a beautiful creek to their right about a hundred fifty feet and a cliff on the left. A trail rule in the Whites is that you should be 200 feet off the trail to camp.

They got close to the creek and found a nice site. Jerry cooked the ramen noodles while Sherry did her regular wipes bath. They ate and Jerry made a good campfire. The creek was giving off pretty music and life was good. Sherry went to gather some fallen fire wood and a lady hiker came by.

Sherry had only met friendly hikers on the AT, so she smiled and greeted the lady. The lady did not smile back. She only said, "you are too close to the trail to camp" and kept on walking. No friendly greeting no good bye. It hurt Sherry's feelings.

Back with Jerry, she told him of the encounter and asked if they should move. "Not unless someone with authority comes by and tells us to. Honey, we are spending the night here. Don't let some snotty lady ruin your evening," was Jerry's response, "Now let's walk over by the creek and enjoy the rest of the evening before we string up the packs and sleep."

There were no other interruptions or hikers and they enjoyed a great night, their first on the AT in the White Mountains.

The next day was a little different. The AMC of New Hampshire had built huts along the trail and they service from thirty-five to sixty hikers. The cost per night is seventy-five dollars and you get a pillow, blanket and bunk space. You also get a very good dinner and a full breakfast. Everything is back-packed in by volunteers daily. No roads reach the huts. The Hermit's hike took them by the Zeeland Falls Hut where they stopped for a break. They were given left over rolls and some good coffee. The volunteers were great folk. There was a bowl for tips, otherwise the left overs were for the hikers.

They took time to sit on the porch and enjoy a gorgeous view then thanked the crew and headed out. It was only a few hundred yards when they began to learn that the Whites were going to live up to their name, tough. In six and a half miles they had climbed Mt. Guyot, and the South Twin Mountain. They had passed the tree line and were close to five thousand feet. Sherry's heels had begun to give her trouble. They were atop the South Twin, a rough top of rabble rock. Some of the rocks were as large as

Cadillacs and others sitting size, so they sat.

Other hikers were around them at a distance. They noticed a father and his young daughter laughing and talking while sharing a small picnic lunch. There were a few others just enjoying the view. Out came the 'Companion, maps and the AT Data Book.' They looked down the South side, practically straight down a quarter mile was Galehead Hut. Jerry said, "Honey, if they have a couple bunks open we will get them for a couple days and give the heels time to rest."

They waited as long as they dared and started down. With bad heels this was no fun. It wasn't long until Jerry knew this was not going to be fun for Sherry, when the back pack came off and she threw it down the mountain. From her position it went about fifty feet down. This was straight down climbing. They finally reached the Galehead Hut to find there was only one bunk spot left and it was the sixth slot up. Sherry said no, she could not handle climbing up that high.

The hut leader explained that they did not

have meals for them but if they were willing to set tables in the morning they were welcome to sleep under the tables in the dining room with the rest of the volunteers. Jerry quickly agreed. They were told they were welcome to use the facilities (no showers available) but potable water. They easily found a spot to fix their supper and enjoyed visiting with the paying customers.

Sleeping on the floor under the tables was a unique experience, and setting the tables was simple. The Hut Leader brought them some fresh baked bread and hot coffee and wished them a good hike and hoped Sherry's heels got better. After finishing the delicious bread and coffee they were off, although much slower.

It wasn't much more than a mile when they came to a side trail, The Gale River Trail. There was a nice spot to sit and relax and they took it. They got out the map to make some decisions. Sherry's heels were killing her. As they sat pondering, a group of girls came up from the

South. Very friendly and excited to be in the wilderness hiking. The troop was ready for a break so they sat around at the trail junction and talked.

Jerry explained the situation, then asked for a consensus as to the roughness of the trail they just came up. Would it be wise for The Overland Hermits to continue on or take this side trail down and call for a shuttle. A spokesman for the girls told him the trail was tough, very tough and the girls all nodded. She suggested it would be the wise thing to take the trail out and live to hike another day.

Jerry thanked them for being honest and said they would take the advice, and abort the hike for now. The break over, the girls all hugged the 'old folk' and headed off just as enthusiastically as they had arrived. Sherry and Jerry stayed awhile longer and talked. Sherry cried, "But I don't want to quit."

"I know you don't, but it is wise to slowly go down the mountain. If necessary we will spend the night, but we should start down."

The 'vitamin I' was kicking in and the trail wasn't rocky, but a good path going down. After an hour they met a team of five volunteers headed up to Galehead Hut with supplies for a couple days. They spoke as they passed but they were loaded and did not want to lose their momentum. Three hours of going down, they came to the trail head. On the bulletin board were numbers for a couple shuttles. In just a few minutes arrangements were made and they sat back on a bench to await their taxi.

Chapter 17

The shuttle took them to the van and wished them well. It was only three o'clock. Nothing much was said on the drive back to Crawford Notch. Jerry noticed tears flowing. He reached over and took her hand and held it until they reached the car. Jerry parked the van and helped

Sherry to a seat in the back. They sat for a long time, and Sherry spoke, "Honey, I'm so sorry. It looks like I was not as ready for this adventure as I thought. I hate to admit it, but I think the Whites may be too much for your old wife." With that effort came more tears and sobs. "What will my friends think after all of my big talk?"

Jerry gave her plenty of time to settle down. After she wiped her eyes and blew her nose, he said, "I remember about the same speech from you when we crashed and burned at Standing Indian. I asked you then how many folk you knew who had backpacked one hundred miles. Now I am going to ask about the same thing. How many people our age do you know that have walked over eighteen hundred miles?............ Sweetheart, we have hiked thru at least twelve states. If we never finish this beautiful trail your friends will say, I could never have done that."

"I know you are right, but for some reason I don't feel a lot better," Sherry sniffed. To Jerry she looked like a school girl.

"Darling, as doctors, we have both lost patients. We fought battles we could never win and we made it through them. This time if we are beat, it is by one of the most beautiful challenges we have ever known. Honey you know that most folks who accept this challenge are whipped within the first couple hundred miles. We have made it over eighteen hundred miles. I feel like we have accomplished a lot. Now let's work on getting your heels in shape before we throw in the towel, what do you say?"

"Thanks for everything Dr. Wiley. You have a great bedside manner and I think I will just kiss you!" And she did.

****

They decided on a motel then dinner. Sherry had looked at the map and picked Gorham, New Hampshire. They were in the motel by 6PM, showered and went out to eat. A big veggie pizza was one of their biggest comfort foods, so it was off to Pizza Hut.

Back in the motel they fixed a chair beside the tub and ran some warm water. Jerry had picked up a box of salt. As her feet soaked they made plans A and B.

Plan A: If the heels were better in 3 or 4 days, they would do some day hikes. One was Rattle River, headed south into the whites. If that worked then North for a few miles toward Maine's Mount Carlo and Goose Eye Mountain. If that worked then sample the trail through Maine and then climb Mount Katahdin.

Plan B: If the heels needed more time they would visit friends in Maine on the way to Bangor and on to Mount Katahdin. If the heels were well enough they would climb it.

Then Jerry suggested plan C. If all else failed, play it by ear. They both got a laugh out of that one.

****

Three days later, with soft insoles, they hiked four miles round trip, starting at the trailhead on US 2 up to the Rattle River Shelter and back.

Sherry felt pretty confident. She also enjoyed talking to the girls scout group they met at the shelter. All the girls were congratulating her for hiking as much of the AT as she had. The trip was a boost to Sherry's peace of mind.

The next day they hiked about the same distance going north. They smiled to see a large cooler about a mile in on the trail. On the top of the chest it said: FOR THRU HIKERS ONLY, ENJOY! Inside was a variety of canned drinks in ice. There was also an attached trash bag. "Trail angels are a special breed," said Jerry.

"They certainly are. It has been heartwarming to see the outpouring along the trail. It renews your faith in humanity," retorted Sherry.

They made a side trip to the top of Mount Washington in the Presidential Range. They drove up and walked to where the AT crosses. Mount Washington experienced the highest recorded winds in the world of 231 mph on April 12, 1934. During the summer, the average temp on Mt. Washington is about fifty degrees. It was an interesting drive to the peak. They were a little disappointed because they had wanted to be hiking over this mountain.

The Hermits drove into Maine, their last state. They towed the car into Maine and hiked up to Old Speck from Grafton Notch. The hike was a little tough, but absolutely beautiful. The two began to think that Maine could match the Whites in many areas.

While hiking through Virginia, the Overland Hermits had met 'Sister Bear and Piper' a couple who were also leap frogging the Trail. They had run into them many times since, sometimes on the trail and other times at trail heads.

After several stops and hiking from trail heads in for a few miles and back out, they came to the small community of Andover Maine. It was such a lovely little community and the Andover General Store and Diner did look inviting. They stopped and had one of the best lobster rolls they had enjoyed since ordering their first on a trip to Nova Scotia. As they sat enjoying the lobster roll, Sherry had to comment on how friendly and outgoing the young lady was that waited on them. It was as if they were in their own home town. "I cannot get over how much my faith in the human race has improved since we started this hike. We have met some wonderful people in this ground pounding eighteen hundred miles.

"Now, let me tell you what I would like to do." Jerry raised his eyebrows and smiled, Sherry continued. "Let's drop back down to highway two and head for Bangor. Sight see a little and let me make sure my heels are as good as I think they are and, if so, let's go to Katahdin and climb it before something else happens to this old body. How about it?"

"Your wish is my command my love. We will do just that and we can tow the car. I had first thought of storing it but, what the heck, we might go on to Canada and not come back this way," Jerry said laughing. They said goodbye to Andover and headed for Bangor.

In Bangor they took a motel, then drove around sightseeing for a while. For dinner, Maine Lobster sounded good. They both enjoyed a pound and a half Maine Lobster and agreed, it was delicious. After dinner they stopped to see the largest wooden statue of Paul Bunyan in the world and then did a little more sightseeing around the thriving city of Bangor. Back at the motel Sherry announced, "I think I am ready. Tomorrow we head for Millinocket then to Baxter State Park for the hike to the summit of Katahdin and the Northern Terminus of the Appalachian Trail."

Maine is a beautiful state and the drive seemed short. Near Baxter State Park they noticed there were no power lines. At the gate they learned that there was a lot more to Baxter than they had known. It was donated to the people of Maine by Governor Percival Baxter. The park was to 'Forever Stay Natural.' Only a few miles of roads are paved. Trails are for hiking, no motorized vehicles allowed on trails. There is no electricity within the park.

On the way to the camping areas they stopped for a few minutes to watch a huge bull moose eating in a lake. They were amazed at the length of time he could keep his head under water to eat the vegetation from the lake bottom.

They chose a campsite at the base of the Abol Trail. They looked at the map and had decided to ascend on Abol and descend on the AT or 'Hunt Trail'. To their surprise, there is no overnight camping on Mt. Katahdin so they would only take a day pack. The brochure said the hike to the summit and back takes an average of eight hours. They decided to have breakfast and leave early.

Chapter 18

They were on the trail at seven o'clock. The Abol trail feels like you are climbing straight up. The trail to the summit is approximately five miles with lots of rocks for footings and also lots of small rocks to act as marbles to help you start back down. The higher they climbed the tougher the climb got. Also the tighter the passage between some huge boulders became. Several times they had to remove the small packs to squeeze through but they were finally climbing Katahdin. They took many breaks and fortunately they had camel back water packs, so it was unlikely they would run out of water. They finally reached the 'Table land'. It took over six hours to reach this flat, rock strewn area of Katahdin. The Abol trail meets the Hunt Trail (AT) on the Table Land.

They met Super Fly, Rawhide, Pedal and Metal coming off the peak. They were all excited to see each other. They had met at a seminar during Trail Days. Pedal told them the mile they had left was a piece of cake, easy walk. That was music to the ears of the Hermits. Super Fly told them that Sister Bear and Piper were at the summit and had told them The Overland Hermits were also climbing today. The four headed on down and Jerry and Sherry headed to their goal.

"Did you tell Sister Bear we were coming up here today?" asked Jerry.

"No, I haven't talked about this decision to anyone."

"Uh oh, I smell a sneaky Dallas Fletcher trick. He is the only one I have mentioned this to. I have a feeling our Sister Bear and Piper are guardian angels sent by the Wiley Industries Corporation." Smiling, Jerry continued, "We will know in about twenty minutes."

"I will say this, I love this trail. I was beginning to wonder as we climbed the Abol," said Sherry, "And I'll bet you are right. I heard Dallas say once, that what happened in the Mediterranean would never happen to their CEO or his wife again."

"I'm not upset. However, I am wondering how many more of our trail mates were undercover for the Company. Dallas is right. Corporate figures, especially wealthy ones, are always targets of people who live off ransoms. Lack of privacy is part of success. Does it bother you honey?"

"No, not in the least. While you were hostage on that yacht in the Med, I spent many hours praying. When the MVA moved in for the rescue I was so relieved. I would accept any loss of privacy to keep that from happening again. So, the answer is NO in capital letters."

Sherry was referring to a terrible incident on their vacation in the Mediterranean where the Yacht they had leased was hijacked by terrorists. Jerry's secret organization, the MVA (Modern Vigilante Association), headed by Jerry's adopted sons, flew over and pulled a miracle out of the hat and rescued Jerry and the yacht crew.

When they reached the famed summit of Katahdin at 5,267 feet the only hikers left at the summit were Sister Bear and Piper. They all greeted and laughed a lot. Sister Bear volunteered to take their victory pictures with the now famous Katahdin peak sign.

After that, they all sat on rocks to talk. "Hey Piper, how long have you guys been working for Dallas?"

"What do you mean Jerry?" Piper said, looking like the cat that had eaten the canary.

"Come on guys, it is hard to put the cat back in the bag once it is out. We are taking a logical guess that Dallas or someone from Wiley Industries has hired you to sorta keep an eye on us. We're not upset. As a matter of fact, we appreciate it."

"Ok, we are busted. You're right, Mr. Fletcher has been in contact with us for years. We have been on retainer. We jumped at this chance."

"That is comforting to know. How did you know Dallas?"

"While you were out saving the world, Sister Bear and I attended your anti-terrorism school there in Pittsburgh. We were FBI then. We are both retired and have wanted to hike this trail for years. This was *a plum assignment*. Now, where are you guys headed from here?"

"We're not telling, you figure it out," said Jerry laughing, "No, we plan to take our time leaving Maine. We might possibly do a little hiking from the trail heads."

"Well, we will try to stay out of your hair, but it may not be as much fun now," laughed Sister Bear.

They talked a little longer, and knowing they were the last to leave the summit, Jerry told the couple to head on down the mountain. He and Sherry were going to sit and enjoy the moment before heading down.

"Well, that was fun," said Sherry, "I really do like them. They sure do know their business."

"Yes, Dallas would only hire the best. Now, let's look around then head back down the AT."

The first mile and a half back down and across the table land was not bad. But the sun was getting near the horizon. Then came some big rocks. As they inched around a boulder on a small ledge they had to climb up to a flat top rock. Two sides of which were straight down, many feet. A touch of fear hit Sherry and she froze. "I can't do this, Jerry." They held the position for a minute. Jerry edged across the crevasse and onto the king rock.

"Hold my hand and do not look down. Crawl onto the rock," urged Jerry. Slowly, Sherry complied, "You have got to do this. It would be tougher to go back down the Abol Trail".

Once on the rock Jerry looked down. The trail was ten feet below him. The trail maintenance crews had drilled and installed one rebar step about six or seven feet down. He explained to Sherry what they would have to do. Again, Sherry said, "I cannot do it, I just can't!"

They sat there for a few minutes. Then Jerry said, as firmly as he could, "I am sliding off the side. When I am down drop both packs and our trekking poles down to me. Then you can do it. Get on your belly and slide off the side of the rock as I do. I will put your feet on my shoulders and step off the rebar and get you down, no sweat." Without waiting for an answer Jerry slid off the rock. His feet hit the rebar and he jumped to the rock below. He took the packs and poles, climbed back up on the rebar and guided Sherry down. There was not a glitch. Sherry was on the next rock, still shaking a little, but felt very safe as she hugged Jerry.

That was the toughest rock. There were more but none that held the possible danger as that owl roost they had been on. In a few hours they were out of the rocks, and on a dirt trail, but it was dark. Once, Sherry slid down. It was an easy fall and she did not get hurt. Jerry had walked on ahead, looked back and Sherry was not attempting to get up. He walked back, "Honey are you hurt?"

"No, but I just want to lay here until daylight." She was resigning.

"That is not an option. You smell like trail mix and some bear or moose will be trying to find it." As Sherry was getting herself together, Jerry walked over to a rock, leaned on his trekking poles to look over the side and he fell. It was an easy fall and only three feet. But, realizing what had happened, his instinct caused him to throw the trekking pole over the mountainside. It had collapsed, broken. Jerry realized just a few hours ago he had trusted those same poles as he leaned on them on the owl roost looking straight down onto rocks about a hundred feet below. He was shaking a little at the realization. He didn't say anything to Sherry.

Their hike was completed in Twenty two hours. The brochure said eight hours. *Maybe we are too old for this*, thought Jerry.

Chapter 19

They took a day at the Abol campsite to sleep and relax. They both still wanted to explore more on the trail. Just south of Katahdin is the area referred to as the *Hundred Mile Wilderness*. It is logging country. That area of the AT has no supply spots and very little access.

They were skipping the Hundred Mile

Wilderness, but they did want to see the town of Monson and other areas south. The roads in northern Maine are private roads, many owned by The Great Northern Paper Company. The company owns over two million acres there. A few roads are blocked off and even charge a fee or toll to use them. Most are unpaved and 'guests' use the roads with the permission of the timber company, but at the driver's risk. The Overland Hermits had no complaints about the roads, and were thankful they were available. The first road they traveled was called the Golden Road. The Golden crosses the Abol Bridge parallel to the AT and they run together for a short while, then the trail veers south into the wilderness. As they drove past the trail head they waved at several hikers emerging from the wilderness, all smiles because they had beat the wilderness and they knew tomorrow they would complete their 2,176 mile odyssey.

The Hermit's aim for today was to drive to the Monson, Maine area. Monson is the southern end of the Wilderness. They found a campsite south of Monson and then toured the little town. While visiting the trail famous 'Monson General Store (and grill)' they had a real home cooked meal. They also met 'Cricket', a sweet young lady who was a solo thru hiker. She only had a little over a hundred miles to go to reach the summit of Katahdin.

After the meal, the Hermits gave Cricket a ride to the trail head and entrance to the Hundred Mile Wilderness. She was all smiles, all five feet of her. She waved and yelled "Thanks again, "as she disappeared into the woods headed for her goal, Mount Katahdin.

Near Caratunk is where the trail crosses the Kennebec River. It is the only river on the trail where a 'ferry' is supplied for all AT hikers. The ferry is a canoe manned by volunteers because there is a danger of the river rising, without warning, from water released up the river.

After walking down to see the ferry area and talking to the volunteer, they decided to hike the

AT a mile or so heading north from the Kennebec. A flier taped to a small tree caught their attention. It was announcing Bill Irwin as a guest speaker at a Caratunk church. The date was yesterday. Jerry was very disappointed. It would have been a chance to meet a legend. The only blind hiker to thru-hike the AT. He and his dog Orient backpacked the entire trail and ascended Katahdin in the snow. The book 'Blind Courage' is Bill's story of the thru-hike. It was one of the Hermit's favorite books.

Back at the van, Jerry fired up his laptop to make an entry into his AOL Journal, 'The Shipslog'. The Shipslog had the privilege of being awarded the Journal of the week, out of the thousands of journals. That night in his entry, he expressed his disappointment in not getting to meet *Bob Irwin*. He published the entry.

In just a few minutes he heard, 'You've got mail.' It was Bill Irwin's wife, Debra. In the e-mail she said his name is Bill Irwin not Bob

Irwin. They communicated back and forth and Jerry apologized for the error. He said he knew the name and had followed Bill's life, bought and read his book. Please let me take you guys to dinner to back up the apology. The net was quiet for a while then she e-ailed back, "We are pretty busy, but thanks."

"Can you believe what I just did?" Jerry said out loud, and Sherry looked up from her book.

"What?"

"I just invited a famous International Motivational Speaker and his wife out to dinner. I am sure he gets thousands of dollars for an hour of his time. What an idiot I am."

"Well darling, even famous people have to eat."

"Quit trying to make me feel better," Jerry laughed.

In a few minutes they heard, 'You've got mail'. It was Debra, Bill's wife again. "If the Overland Hermits will let Bill pick the place either in Dover-Foxcroft or Bangor. He accepts your invitation."

"Of course," Jerry said, "Anywhere will be fine." Bill picked Bangor for the coming Friday evening, two days away.

What an evening. Bill was gracious, explaining why he wanted to pick the place. He was now a vegan. Debra is a beautiful lady and very sweet. Bill's dog, Orient, was retired and he had a new dog. Jerry mentioned how mannerly the dog was. Bill's comment with a smile was, "Jerry, she is working now."

It was an evening they would never forget. Bill and Debra were building a house on a mountain with a full view of Katahdin, Bill had said, "Even though I cannot see it, I enjoy the view." He laughed and they all joined in.

After dinner they went outside to give the Hermits an opportunity for pictures. Debra retrieved them an autographed copy of Bill's book entitled "Orient, Dog Guide of The Appalachian Trail". As Debra drove away Jerry took note of the car tag, ORIENT. He smiled.

"Now, that is something I never expected to happen," said Jerry. "To actually meet Bill Irwin and enjoy the enthusiasm he and Debra exude. No wonder he is in such demand as a speaker. What a thrill!"

After such a high, driving out of the parking lot, Jerry spotted what he now had begun to look for, and he waved. Piper waved from a dark corner of the parking lot. Jerry drove close and got out. He walked over and notified Sugar Bear and Piper of their plans to visit friends in Kennebunk Port and Scarborough then head home.

Jerry had guessed that Dallas had dispatched friendly troops as security if they were to need it. The Hermits did learn they had been very well protected. Blaze, Little Forest, Moonshine and Pickle along with the two couples Chilly Willy & Just Ray and Sugar Bear and Piper were all agents of Wiley Industries to act as protection for the Overland Hermits.

Sherry and Jerry had agreed after this dinner they would drop this great adventure and file it under 'we took our best shot.'

Over the next few days they enjoyed time with friends. Neither had regrets. It had been an adventure that required cooperation. A part of marriage that cements a union. So even in their seventies, they had enjoyed hiking with some wonderful folks on the AT. Knowing the Appalachian Trail Community will change a life forever. Life is good, enjoy it.

ABOUT THE AUTHOR

Jack served honorably in the USMC, USAF and USN. He retired as a chief petty officer, his last assignment was teaching Naval Intelligence Processing. He is also a licensed general contractor.

As a professional chalk artist and story teller, Jack and Sherry, his wife, have entertained audiences from Cuba to Canada, appearing at churches, youth camps and BSA functions. After hundreds of stories orally, Jack is now committing some of his stories to paper. Recording these stories has become a rewarding hobby.

Late in life he and his wife hiked nearly 2,000 miles on the Appalachian Trail. Their hike began at Springer Mountain in Georgia and ended for them in New Hampshire. Leg injuries prevented completion of the final miles. They still dream.

This book is a result of those dreams. Although the novel is fiction, the facts and most incidents recorded actually happened. Having dinner with Bill Irwin and his wife Debra was an actual happening, as described in the book.

Jack and his wife Sherry travel full time in their motor home. Through all fifty states and to twenty-six countries, life has always been an adventure. The two adventures top the list. One, hiking the AT and the other the drive North Carolina to Alaska. The couple has crisscrossed the USA from San Diego, California to Nova Scotia and from Key West, Florida to Alaska. Their odyssey together began September 1956.

Sherry & Jack Darnell at Katahdin's peak. The white blaze under the sign is the final blaze of the AT

Personal From the Author

The Appalachian Trail leaves so many memories one could never list them all. We met hikers from at least ten countries and most states. We actually hiked into a Surprise Birthday party for 'Pigpen'. She was waylaid at a Shelter by her family. Hiker Mark, walked up on a wedding at one of the Balds on the trail. We saw goats, deer, bear, fox, elk and moose on the trail. We met doctors, nurses, preachers, college students, seniors (one lady alone in the 100 mile wilderness was 83). We hiked with a professor (Gordy), met a pilot who was a close friend of John Denver and a fire chief. It would be impossible to list them all, but if you hike the AT, your faith in the human race will be boosted.

*********** *********** ***********

Trail Names of Hikers we have met:

This first list is of Hikers we met when we were acting as trail angels in the 'Hundred Mile Wilderness':

Bott (M. Marshall), Builder (Mark Darnell-NC), Cornish (Murray of Australia), Freeman (Switzerland), Hiker Ike (PA), Honeymoon Hikers (Walk with Jesus), Lady (SC), Late-For-Dinner, Preacher Man (R. Sears, Memphis), Tina Castle (DC), Two Berries, Just Two Ladys (Swiss), Zeke (Bryant Amper). We also met a husband,wife and adult daughter from Denmark who were hiking and did not have trail names.

The following Trail names are only a few met on the trail:

All Balls, Andy. April, Arrow, Badger, Barking Spider, Bealu, Big Foot, Big Red, Boats, Blaze (USMC)Semper Fi, Blue Heron, Blueberry, Bonzi, Brownstone, Bucky, Cash, Cacotopia, Chief, Chief & Mischa, Chilly Willie and Just Ray, Christopher, Robin, Christ opus, Clorox, Clserdia (Denmark), Coffee Head, Condo, Cricket, Crispy, Cube Star, Cucaracha, Dan, Dragon Fly, Daydreamer, Devine, Doggy Boy, Double Barrel, Dr. Bud and Spud, Drufus, Dude, Easter Bunny, e-Bunny, Fire fly, Flame, Flying Scot (Scotland), Freedom, Gangsta, Girl, Good Indian, Gordy, Granny, Grey Owl (coffee), Gucci Man, Gucci Woman, Gunslinger, Gunslinger (2), Half Pint and Freight Train, Hamster Head, Hawk, Hayes, He Man, Head, Herald, Hemlock, Herbie and I, Hitching Post (Seattle), Hollywood, Hondo Mama, Hyper man, In-Tents, Jeff , Jello, Jennice, Jessie JO JO , Miley, John, Johnny J, Jolly Roger, Jumpstart and Belau, Junker, Just Don, Keeper, Kentucky Rifle, Kentucky Slim, Kentucky Dude, Lauren, Lexan, Lightening Bold (NC), Lite Brite, Little Forest, Lizard, Louisville and Plugger, Lynn, Madam Little, Malibu Barbic, Malibu Barbie, Man with Dog,

Mat, Midwest Wind and Mischa, Mollie Moon Beam, Moon Child, Moonshine, Moses, Mr Snake (MI), Mr. Pink, Mr. President, Nature Boy, PAHA, Paint Brush, Pan, PAPA Smurf, Paris, Pat & Annie, PatchFoot, Paul & Jean, Pedal and Metal, Penguin (South Africa), Periwinkle, Pickle, Pig Pen (AT Birthday party), Pilgrim, Pipe Wrench, Piper the Cub, Plaid Shirt, Polish Ninja, Pup, Rain Drop, Raindog, Ramblin Man, Rawhide, Red Hat and Sugarbear, Rev, River Rat, Rock Top, Rocky Top (2), Salamander, Santiago, Scare Crow (Africa), Seaweed, Seven Layer Burrito, Silk, Sir Richard (England), Sister Bear, Sister Bear & Piper, Skate, Skypilot, Skyscrape, Skywalker, Sleepy, Slips, Smooch (UK), Snafu, Snake, Sparrow, Stagerlee, Starburst, Steam Shovel, Stone Brown, Stout, Sunshine. Super Fly, Sweet Pea, The Carnaval (3 girls), The Chief, The Good Nurse, The Rock, The Virginian, Tia, Tin Man & Godiva, Tinman #2, Toast, Tonto, Trekking Pole (Poland), Trip and Arby, Troll, Turkey Bacon, Twinkle Toes, Two Scoops, Two Scoops (2), Uncle Ralph, Uncle Walt, Valleygirl, Viking, Wags, Walkabout, Weather Carrot, Whisper, White Bread, Willie, Wizard, Wizard (2), Woodman, Wreck, Wrecker, Yetti, Reb (USMC).

Other books by Jack Darnell

Sticky
Rags
S'gar
Finally Love
Mary Ann
The Vacation
Why Not Forever
Gracefully Grasping For Dignity
Toby's Tales
(Available as paperback and e-books)

http://shipslog-jack.blogspot.com/

Jacsher@aol.com

www.ingramcontent.com/pod-product-compliance
Lightning Source LLC
Chambersburg PA
CBHW020240130626

46549CB00005B/1989